Before Hiroshima:
The Confession of Murayama Kazuo
and other stories

Joshua Barkan

Before Hiroshima:
The Confession of Murayama Kazuo
and other stories

The Toby Press, *London*

First published in 2000 by
The Toby Press *Ltd, London*
www.tobypress.com

'Before Hiroshima' first appeared in *News From the Republic of Letters.*

ISBN 1 902881 08 7 (C)
ISBN 1 902881 13 3 (PB)

A CIP catalogue record for this title is available from the British Library

Designed by Fresh Produce, London

Typeset in Garamond by
Rowland Phototypesetting Ltd., Bury St Edmunds

Printed and bound in Great Britain by
St Edmundsbury Press Ltd., Bury St Edmunds

For Laura

Contents

Before Hiroshima:

The Confession of Murayama Kazuo

T615 Kyoto-ken
Kyoto-shi
2–3-12 Kawaramachi-cho
Murayama Kazuo

July 25, 1995

T112 Tokyo-ken
Tokyo-shi
5–6-19 Shinjuku
Mizuoshi Hideoki

Dear Mizuoshi-san,

As the fiftieth anniversary of the Hiroshima atomic bomb massacre approaches, I am struck by the recent death of your father and your grandfather. During the war your grandfather served as my commanding officer and the news of his plane crash, which I read about only this morning, reminds me of the danger of unwanted surprises. It causes me to realize that I, too, may soon be forced to leave this world.

Perhaps it may be of some comfort that your grandfather attained so much success before his death. The picture of his funeral motorcade in the paper is quite impressive. I did not know he had been commissioned a general and that he had been elevated to a seat in the Diet. In fact, I have not spoken to your grandfather or heard from him since the end of the war. Still, the shock of his death prompts me to write to you immediately. For in thinking about your grandfather, and the benevolent image reported of him in the paper, I am afraid he may not have told you or anyone else much about the war—and certainly not about my error.

Or perhaps I should say our error. For without wishing to shock you, I believe I know a very different side of the man whom you knew as your grandfather.

It comes to me now that, perhaps, I should not be writing this letter to you. Please forgive me. I do not wish to hurt you. I know you must be mourning deeply and that you must have little time for memories of an era which surely seems long ago. But if I do not write this letter to you, then to whom should I write? (For I cannot bring myself to confess my error to my family. There are some things which can only be told to a stranger, as with a drunk neighbor in a yakitori bar.) And if I do not reveal my secret I am afraid I will die with a thick blackness inside my heart, most probably as your grandfather died, too; though I am sure he saw the past differently from me. Please listen to me then. I beg you. For without wishing to aggrandize myself, I believe I could have saved the lives of every one of those who perished in Hiroshima and Nagasaki.

Let me say first that I was an officer at the time, at the end of the war. Not a high level officer, but not an insignificant fish either. I was twenty-two, a captain, and second in

4

command of the central intelligence gathering post in the old Nijo Palace of Kyoto, where I had begun my military career the second year of the Pacific War.

Remarkably enough the palace looked quite grand then. The pebbles on the walkways surrounding the grounds were always raked. The pine trees that fringed the moss garden and the central pond were pruned every season, and each morning a group of twenty soldiers shined the cedar floorboards inside the palace until every grain of wood rippled in its natural form. Such attention, of course, was quite unusual during the last days of the war. Supplies and especially manpower were short, and the enemy's bombers threatened constantly to destroy our buildings. The army and navy had already been beaten everywhere or were in retreat. The situation was quite grave. (If I am mentioning details which you are already aware of please forgive me. But I am not sure of your age. In fact, the thought that you are younger than twenty, or even thirty, motivates me in part to write this letter. Certainly it requires me to relate this memory clearly. For I am afraid history is not being taught well in our schools these days.)

By now, of course, as you may have guessed, the care given to the palace was no accident. It was the will of my commander, the first-in-charge of everyone, Mizuoshi-san. Dressed in his crisp gray uniform—which he always had starched and creased twice before placing it over his thick, powerful body—and framed by his sword, his riding whip, his black polished leather boots, and his perfectly cropped half-length mustache (which he grew down to the edges of his fat lips), he caused the underlings to run simply by the sound of his officious strides pressing into the white gravel of the Nijo court. Unlike most of the soldiers, whom he regularly berated as weak, Mizuoshi-san had never been drafted. In 1920 he joined the Imperial Army, and then—as he liked to constantly remind me—it was only after he had worked his way through the ranks, after he had learned the true hard meaning of fighting in Korea, Manchuria, and Nanking, that he was promoted and sent to Kyoto. Mizuoshi-san was never to be spoken to until he had spoken first.

I remember once, for example, during my first few days at headquarters, I rushed up to him with the news of our brilliant victories in the Philippines. The palace floorboards creaked wildly as I hurried toward his inner sanctum. I could not contain my excitement as I burst into his office. "We have had success," I said firmly. "We have had success." Mizuoshi-san grabbed the cable from me and put on his thick, heavy, glasses. He scrutinized the teletype then gave it back to me. "Yes, it *is* good news," he replied at last. His lips parted half way into a smile, revealing his crooked yellow teeth. (Some had been badly capped in the peasant village where he grew up. He looked truly like a rice farmer, which is what, as you must already know, he had been as a child.) "Yes . . . But you should not have spoken to me first. A young officer must learn respect and discipline the same as a fresh and ignorant soldier . . . Especially if the officer is fresh and ignorant himself." Mizuoshi-san looked at me long and hard with his obsidian

6

eyes. "The memory of your great grandfather will not help you here. It does not matter if you are the grandson of the former general, you must earn your rank now." He turned back to his meticulously organized desk. "You will not eat the next five days," he ordered. I bowed deeply. And though I thought he was wrong not to have recognized the special circumstances which had caused me to commit my error, I did not eat the next five days.

I remember it was two years later on the sixth of June, 1945, when I noticed an intelligence wire of interest as it came into our command post. I was in the decoding room; it was three in the morning and the teletype machine was tapping lightly. The night was calm, and for some reason Kyoto had not yet been bombed during the war, so people slept without much fear of air raids. (Wild theories circulated on the streets that our city was safe because of protective spirits or because the Emperor would not permit such a beautiful city to be destroyed. But we in the intelligence community explained such a calculated error as propaganda to convince the people that they should surrender, to make them believe the Americans would not be cruel victors: though, how then could the regular fire bombings of Tokyo be explained?)

Anyway, I was quite drowsy that night, and the hot summer air and the sound of crickets mixing with the light tapping of the teletyper did nothing to keep me awake. Mizuoshi-san insisted I stay up the four nights a week when we received summaries of the enemy's activities from our outposts. The transmissions were sent at night because the enemy was asleep then, unlikely to be monitoring us. Or so, at least, Mizuoshi-san repeatedly argued they might be.

Of course there was no real reason why I had to be in the decoding room as the messages came in. I could just as easily have received them in the morning, as Mizuoshi-san did from me. Any of the intelligence operators could have warned us if something was urgent, and none of the others had to stay up each night, they rotated. But the one time I made this observation to Mizuoshi-san, he just laughed. "You still have much to prove," he barked loudly enough for the other lower ranking officers nearby to hear.

On the night of the sixth, then, I was reading each report as it came in, searching for any sign out of the ordinary, though my eyes were closing. The bombings were continuing in Osaka, Kobe, Nagoya, Himeji and Wakayama. One of our intelligence posts had been moved from Osaka to our own at the end of the fourth year of the war, the attacks were so ferocious there. Few cities of importance had not yet been bombed by the end of the war, and most of the secondary targets had been touched or destroyed as well. Numbers and symbols dashed across the brown paper in the teletype machine. The class of each group of bombers was cited, the quantity of planes, the height of enemy strikes and the success of any of our anti-aircraft fire as well as the calculated weight of bombs dropped and the expected damage. As the sheets jerked forward I scanned each list. By this time in the war the code was second nature to me. Nevertheless, the rhythm of the teletyper was too hypnotizing for me to force any careful scrutiny until morning, no matter how hard I tried.

And yet, although the jumble was too dense to dissect rapidly, a large number suddenly stood out from among the other slashes and dots, characters, parentheses and stars, as if a drop of blood shining brightly, fresh vermilion, in a field of snow. A bomb weighing an estimated two thousand three hundred kilos—a single bomb—had been dropped over Kobe near the center of the harbor, with only a few other smaller accompanying bombs. I put on my glasses and studied the number. Perhaps I had misread the zeros behind the twenty-three. I ordered Takayama over, one of the two other operators in the room who had been playing cards during the print-out, and asked him to look at the number too. He confirmed the figure and I told him to wire the source in Kobe. The source repeated the information, adding a damage description with a note that the planes which dropped the bomb had been flying very high when the bomb was released. The source asked for any action to take. I replied none at the moment but that someone would be down the next day to inspect the site. A few minutes later I put on my cap, and I combed my hair with my fingers. I rubbed the sleep out of my eyes and kneaded my cheeks to regain some color. I hurried to the far end of the palace, through the dark rooms of the old Shogun Ieyasu's meeting halls and across the various other inner courtly chambers. The palace was silent and delicate. The flower arrangements, scrolls, screen paintings, swords and cushions were all neatly ordered and faintly glowing in the bluish-white moonlight, yet there was a firmness too, a solidity to the wooden floorboards. Near Mizuoshi-san's chamber I slowed until I could no longer hear my footsteps. Mizuoshi-san insisted I report everything significant to him immediately. At least six or seven times before I had woken him up, after the first surprise bombing of Tokyo for example. Usually, I knocked on his paper door firmly but softly, then I waited in his hallway until he put on his nemaki coat, and then he ordered me in. But on this night I hesitated before knocking. A powerful smell of sake emanated from his room, and I knew he did not usually drink but that when he did he did not stop until he passed out. I turned to leave, but "Who's there?" he shouted. The floorboards had creaked. "It's me," I said hoarsely. I cleared my throat. "Why didn't you identify yourself earlier?" I knew he wanted no response so I waited quietly outside. At last, he opened his screen door, but unlike the other times he did not invite me in. He stood face to face with me, a few raw gray whiskers sticking out, highlighted by the moon. His firm jaw and heavy chest—covered with a stained undershirt—poked toward my skinny frame. His cheeks were red. Sharp lines ran across his sleep-creased face. "What is the news?" he demanded. "A large bomb has been dropped over Kobe. The flight pattern of the enemy is unusual." "What was destroyed?" "An area the size of fifty-two normal bombs. An entire long dock with a matériel shed and small barracks." Mizuoshi-san breathed heavily into my face. "And this is why you have come to me in the middle of the night?" I bowed like a dog trying not to be caned. "For false reports?" My lips tightened, my face still down. "I am sorry to have disturbed you," I said. "I did not want to bother you, but the source in Kobe confirmed the report." Mizuoshi-san stumbled closer to me. He spoke with slurred yet sharp speech. "Then the source in Kobe has confirmed an error twice." Spit flew from his lips onto my forehead and he tugged my ear until it stung. He staggered back and shut his door. I inched away from his chamber quietly. And then I moved to my own quarters to nurse my ear in cold water and to sleep.

The next morning I awoke on my mat. The weave of the old floor grass was splitting. I slept alone in a room in the ancient servant quarters, a series of wooden boxes where many of the other soldiers slept, too, but in groups. Mizuo-shi-san's chamber lay on the opposite side of the palace. The sun had come up recently but the sky was brownish gray, and by the looks of it the weather was going to stay that way a couple of days. I sprawled on my back and studied the small holes in the ceiling where termites had eaten. Twice, Mizuoshi-san had told us to exterminate them, but we had no chemicals. The other soldiers were still asleep and I had at least an hour before I needed to report to Mizuoshi-san. I wondered how I could get to Kobe to see the effects of the giant bomb. Certainly the bomb did not seem like an insignificant development to me.

My first plan was to lie that my mother was sick. Our family-house hugged the southern road out of town towards Osaka bay. But visits to families for sentimental reasons were almost impossible at the time, even to see a mother. Nearly everyone had someone killed or dead at home, so what was the importance of a sick mother?

The second possibility, of course, was to investigate another report and then to divert my path. But whoever went with me as my assistant—and there was always an assistant—would suspect the change in orders and they might report me to Mizuoshi-san. Moreover, there was no other highly significant bit of news near Kobe, and usually we did not follow up information ourselves, we relied on further details from our sources. After all, that was why we had outlying contacts. The trip might be too long to come back in a day, too, depending on road conditions. Yet despite all these problems this option seemed the best to me if I could choose my assistant.

An hour later I reported for duty, to where Mizuoshi-san was surveying the main office, planted in the center of the room. Twenty-six soldiers toiled at their desks, flipping through files, scribbling annotations across their papers or calculating the meaning of each crisis. Occasionally one of them rushed to the decoding room to obtain further information. Our two youngest soldiers copied each final report by hand at their small desks in the corner of the room. The official records stacked up like bricks in brown folders on every desktop. The desks were aligned in perfect rows. I marched up to Mizuoshi-san to request permission to inspect reports of sabotage at the railroad connection just north of Osaka. Mizuoshi-san's face was pale and gaunt. He had managed to shave, of course, but he had cut himself.

His eyes were still glassy and he looked more sedate than usual so I gained some confidence. I stepped closer to him and bowed. But suddenly, although he was out of his ordinary, busy, character, I could not help but notice that his posture was as firm as ever. His body was immense. He was like a stone wall. I could have punched him with all my might and he would barely have moved. For more than a minute I waited for him to let me speak, but he did not acknowledge me. He grabbed a report from an assistant as he walked by and studied it. After five minutes I could no longer stand there. My legs shook. I bowed and turned to walk to my desk. "What do you want?" Mizuoshi-san asked me when I was half way to my seat. The operators nearby glanced up from their work. I turned back toward Mizuoshi-san, and there he was, still, his short cropped gray hair, his thick-skinned face, his squinting eyes. "Nothing," was all I could say. "I wanted nothing, sir." I bowed lower. "You have made me tired," he growled. The soldiers returned to their reports. I pushed my head deeper and stumbled back to my seat. I tried to concentrate on my papers but I was unable to focus my eyes. Mizuoshi-san remained in the center of the room and I did not move. At last, however, I stood, and I spoke to him in an unusually high voice. "Commander, there is another report which I did not mention to you last night. The railroad at Osaka is indicating further signs of sabotage. Permission is requested to inspect the problem." Mizuoshi-san's face tightened and his cheeks turned red. He spoke in a low yet charged voice. "Yes, it *is* still a problem. But it is an insignificant matter and you know it. The misdeed will soon be rectified when the bandits are caught." He pounded toward his office. "Your desire to inspect stems from laziness." He stopped suddenly, however, and twisted back to me. "But you should learn what war is really like. You should learn to do something more than fill papers. Go, and leave me alone."

By the time I arrived in Kobe it was late in the afternoon. I had hurried as much as I could in Osaka, and I did not need to investigate much there. (The police were quite efficient during the war. They had rounded up a group of saboteurs from the usual informants—housewives in various buildings.) Yet despite my speed, the road from Osaka to Kobe was slow, and Matsubara my assistant had to drive around deep pot-holes filled with murky oil-stained water. The gutters along the road stank from bodies and aban-doned shoes and clothing. Families had dropped the articles or worn them out as they fled to the countryside. The sludge of wet rags had developed into a sickly brown color which I found hard to look at. (How many people had left everything only to eat grass in the countryside?) Burnt trucks and cars hulked at almost every pull-over. Occasionally, a pile of dead bodies mounded, jumbled together, ready for burning. The cause of death was unidentifiable by looking at the pale and blotchy limbs, but most died of dysentery and hepatitis. It was the absence of movement, the silence of their bodies which weighed like an anchor on everything around them, and I could not speak to Matsubara whenever we passed the corpses.

At last we arrived at the site of the bomb near the north end of the Kobe harbor. The source, a tiny old man, Tojio-san, met us and Matsubara parked our jeep as close to the waterfront as possible. The concrete had buckled into giant blocks around the edge of the dock. The ground was broken up almost everywhere else along the harbor too. A long line of battered shipping cranes and flattened metal sheds, severed brick chimneys, and crumbled walls jutted into the water, receding into the distance around the bay. Dust covered the waterfront in an ash-white film. The loading docks were as noiseless and void as a cemetery in winter. The city looked abandoned—the citizens inside, it seemed, for fear of air raids. Yet behind me, I could hear the voices of men and women shouting. And there, in the near distance when I turned, were twenty or thirty adults and children picking through a field of rubble as large as an aircraft carrier. They hollered as if searching for bodies, calling for anyone who might be able to respond. "Over there," Tojio-san said. "That is where the explosion happened." He swung his arms wildly back and forth as he pointed. "It is nothing now. Nothing more than pieces." His eyes were red from crying, but he restrained his tears. "The navy barracks were at the far end of the matériel shed. A friend of mine managed the dock, but he is dead now. We found most of the bodies yesterday, but there are still more to recover."

A few minutes later, as I stepped onto the rubble, I had the odd sensation of standing where something else had existed only recently before. (As I grow older I have become acutely aware that the difference between being and not being is extremely small. Who, for example, will remember us when we are gone?) The concrete, rock and metal shards punched at the soles of my boots. "What should we do?" Tojio-san demanded. He scurried beside me, his steps half the length of mine. We scrambled up and down over the scattered mounds of decimated material. "We do not know how it could have happened so fast. It was such a big bomb. We have never seen such a big explosion." He shook his head. His neck was wrinkled, and I slowed for him to keep pace. He looked like most of the volunteers at the end of the war: older than sixty, a veteran of other battles. After all, most of the young men my age had already died. Detritus surrounded us like a left-over stew. Scraps of wide-barreled guns and tanks, rubber tires, and steel innards poked through smaller more rounded pieces of concrete and rock. From the top of a particularly large heap I gazed across the no man's land. The blast was perfectly circular. The edge of the explosion halted abruptly in a black line, far in the distance, and I could barely see the fringe. I turned around and around, unable to absorb the immensity of the explosion. I strained my sight, trying to see the whole field of the bomb at once. I shook my head and felt the need to sit down. I must have looked extremely small in the middle of the flattened ruin. There was only one crater, which eliminated the possibility of multiple bombs; but the depression was surprisingly shallow for such a large detonation. "And you saw the explosion?" I asked the source at last. I did not know what difference it would make if he had. I knew only the basics of interrogation and little about bombs, but I had studied the work of other officers—including, even, Mizuoshi-san—and I had become aware that the smallest bits of evidence could quickly become consequential later. "No, I just heard it. It was a boom. A loud boom. Everyone in the city must have heard it. Even the rice farmers on the other side of the hill." Tojio-san glanced at the mountains above the town. "But you did not see it?" I asked. "No. I was eating yakitori in Kurashima's," Tojio-san laughed, lowering his head to his feet. "Drinking beer too?" I demanded. (Only the corrupt had alcohol or chicken at the end of the war. Everyone else ate rice or nothing.) I scrutinized him and fiddled with my officer's cap. He hurried across the rubble field to an old woman and tore her away from where she was shouting, wailing a funeral dirge at the ground. The woman rushed up to me still hunched from the search and from arthritis, too, no doubt. She was crying, but she wiped away her tears immediately. A tattered straw-farmer's hat covered her dyed black hair, and a light blue dirty rag secured the hat, tied around her chin. Deep wrinkles cut across her forehead; the lines were filled with ash and grime, and she had dark blue work pants on. "Oh officer-san. I am so sorry I did not come sooner. I saw the explosion! I saw it!" She bowed again and again, shaking her head back and forth, as if begging forgiveness for any inconvenience she might have caused me. I bowed and waited until she could breathe more freely. "What did you see?" I asked. "I was over there when it happened. Yes. Over there." She refused to look at me as she spoke. "On the hill. Yes. My husband works in the matériel shed and I was bringing him lunch. It was twelve o'clock and he prefers hot rice. Oh yes, he does not like it cold." "And you did not hear the air-raid warning?" "Oh no. There was no siren!" She covered her ears. "I was in the middle of the street. Just in the middle." She waved toward the road up the hill, at the main street which led to the center of town, to a place no more than four hundred meters away. "And you did not see any planes? Nothing?" (How could I force her to remember? How could I have been so cruel? But a feeling of strength, of commanding passed through me, the warmth of astuteness, of solving a problem.) "Yes, I saw three planes. There were three of them." She beat her chest. "There were three evil American planes, and I did not think they could harm me." She clenched her fist at the sky. "They were going somewhere else, I thought. They were not like the usual planes. Oh no. They were just tiny dots. Shimmering. High. Going somewhere else." She threw her head back and looked at the sky. "That's when I heard a whistle and the planes cut sharply away. They disappeared and the whistle grew louder and I ran. But the whistle shrieked so loud I knew it would hit me. I threw my hands over my head. 'Now I am dead,' I thought. 'Now I am going to die.' But the bomb exploded in front of me, above the ground, and I fell back. I tried to stand but it was useless. I dropped the rice." The woman wiped her dusty hands against her faded work pants and looked away from me. "Over there," she pointed. "My husband must be in the corner, over there. Near the gate.

Or where it was. That is where he always came to meet me." Her body shook and I turned to Tojio-san. "Put everyone near the gate to search. Find her husband," I commanded. Tojio-san ran through the crowd, yelling at the searchers to move to the site of the gate. After that, I could not stand on the mound much longer. I needed fresh air. The smell of dead bodies rose from the ruins. Pieces of corpses and tanks swirled in a collage. I bowed to the woman, and she bowed lower to me. "Oh, thank you, officer-san. Thank you. You must learn to stop the bombs! You must learn to stop them! We are counting on you for your leadership." She scurried across the rubble field to where the other searchers were gathered.

Back at the jeep I paced along the desolate shoreline, wondering how a single bomb could have been so powerful, while Matsubara waited in the staff car. Matsubara ran his fingers up and down the steering wheel. I contemplated the dead. I contemplated the giant circle of the bomb. I contemplated the shallow crater. And when I could come up with no solution we began the long return to head-quarters, back to Mizuoshi-san.

Had I not been with Matsubara I would have insisted we make it to headquarters that night no matter how difficult the road conditions, but Matsubara was my favorite assis-tant. He never asked why I wanted to go to Kobe. He had simply inquired what we were going to do there. Before leaving Kyoto I had warned him we might have to return late, but he had simply replied, "It is horrible when the engine breaks down on an important trip, leaving a person stranded for a day or two. Don't you think?" His humor shone brightly when he let it, despite his reticence.

As we drove back the sky stayed lit until almost ten. It was still the beginning of summer, though the clouds reminded me more of winter. Eventually, the heavens darkened, and our yellow headlights carved only a tiny pocket into the night. Cicadas and tree frogs croaked mournfully by the side of the road. They had multiplied with the funguses and with every kind of plague as the number of dead rose. (Writing to you now, I am struck by the imbalance of the world that evening. There are some—biologists and Buddhist priests, for example—who would argue that plants and animals must grow as fast as they decay, that the way of the universe is the cycle of life and death, that the laws of nature were simply being fulfilled that evening as smoothly and constantly as an equation. But it was *we* who were causing the bodies to be precipitously destroyed. Flies and mold grew phenomenally during those days. And perhaps we would have realized our error sooner if we had only been allowed to study true religion.) The jeep bumped up and down over potholes and I began to close my eyes; I suspected Matsubara wanted to sleep too, but there was nowhere convenient to stop. "Can you make it near to Kyoto?" I asked Matsubara. He nodded and shifted gears extra-smoothly to save gas and to even out the ride. I slept for a few hours, placing complete trust in him.

When we were fifteen kilometers from Kyoto, Matsubara woke me gently. "Murayama-san, we are near the city. Where is the turnoff exactly?" I started as I awoke and looked around. The steep hills of my childhood surrounded us. The road was the color of blood iron. "Up ahead. A few more kilometers. Take the first right towards Minami-ku. The house is on the hill, near the top of the road, just before the village."

Between the uneven highway and my dreams, I had not slept well. I had imagined air raids against Kyoto, the city splattered in fire from no more than a few hundred of the Kobe-type bombs. The giant pagoda of the Toji-dera and the cherry-blossomed hills of the Kiyomizu-temple lay in cindered ruins. Matsubara pulled our jeep off the main road and we climbed the old peasant path toward Minami-ku. The trail switched back and forth. Sharp bamboo leaves canopied the road, blowing and scratching in the wind. The branches swayed darkly. It was too opaque to see them clearly, but they emitted a presence like a closed door at night which cannot be seen but only felt. And like a door, they seemed to hide the world above from the war-pocked road below. The air blew warmer, more familiar, beyond the curtain of bamboo. The jeep tires cut into the mud pushing us toward my home. "Cut left onto the gravel driveway," I told Matsubara near a particularly sharp switch-back. We rolled to the end of the long path and stopped abruptly in front of my grandfather's moss-covered old goldfish pond. "Turn off the engine," I whispered. It was long past midnight and the lanterns inside the house were out.

I did not shut my door as I leapt from the jeep to stretch and to smell the familiar odors of my home more closely. Two years had passed since the last time I had traveled home.

Matsubara cut the lights and darkness enveloped the wooden walls of my house again. I eased across the narrow flagstone path to the front door, feeling my way across each slippery stone by memory. I inched up the front three steps and removed my shoes, then slid the paper door open a centimeter at a time. A swift current of hot air burst through the door. Faint smoke from the kitchen fireplace mixed with the rich smell of the giant, ancient, cedar beams which supported the roof. I smelled dust too: the house was still uninvaded by soldiers and troops who scrubbed floors each morning, and I breathed deeply. I snapped my fingers at Matsubara and he followed, tiptoeing along the wet path, trying not to fall.

"Who's there?" a high-pitched woman's voice shouted suddenly. The woman descended the steps from upstairs carrying a big stick. "It's me. Put that away," I whispered. "You who!?" The woman tilted her head down to the side as if attempting to cut the angle to see me better. She held her stick firmly. At least she seemed to. Nothing was clear. Silhouettes flashed. Black movement. "It's me. Your nephew," I said. It was my aunt from Tokyo, I realized at last. "Kazuo?" she asked. "Kazuo, is that really you?" She nearly fell. She threw her hands to her forehead, dropping her stick, and ran to the bottom of the steps, then up to me. For a moment she studied me, circling me, touching my uniform, smiling. "You are alive! You are still in this world!" "Yes. I'm safe in Kyoto. Of course! Hasn't Mother told you? She must have." "Yes, I know. I know. But you are here. You are proof. I do not trust the letters I get from Haruo. Every sheet is like a phantom, and one day I will get no letter. But you are here." She laughed, wincing a little, and wiped away her tears. "Come. You must be hungry. I'll get you some food." She stepped lightly toward the kitchen, looking for a lantern. "What are you doing here?" I whispered. "When did you come?" I followed her into the cooking area while Matsubara waited outside on the front porch, although I tried to pull him in. "We are all here now. Nine of us. Everyone's upstairs. The four of us, your mother, your grandfather, your father's sister, Michiko and Sachiko. We came this week. There is nothing left for us in Tokyo or in Yokohama." She lit a lantern and orange light wobbled around the kitchen. Ashes smoldered in the cooking area and small wisps of smoke drifted up the chimney. Cast iron pots still hung from the ceiling, but there were many fewer, perhaps they had been sold. In a moment I heard footsteps rushing behind me, down the staircase, and then the sweet flowing voice of my mother. "Kazuo! Oh, Kazuo! Son. My son." My mother burst into the kitchen. She was crying and she lowered her head so I would not see her tears. "I knew I heard something! I knew it." She was wearing her red yukata, the one I always loved as a child. "You must forgive me," my aunt said. "I thought you were a thief. There have been bandits lately. It is all they talk about in the village." My mother pressed my face into her breast and kissed me. She rocked me back and forth. She ran her fingers through my hair and under my officer's cap. "I'll find some vegetables," my aunt said. "Maybe even a scrap of meat." "You are here!" my mother whispered. She stroked my head.

"Yes, you are here," a deep cracking voice echoed from the kitchen doorway. I jerked my head up, bumping my mother's chin. And there was my grandfather, dressed in his large gray kimono, the one which fanned around his legs and hugged his shoulders tightly. His belt was cinctured crisply around his waist, and his collar was starched. He had waited, clearly, until he was dressed to descend. His head shone balder than I remembered it, but his hair had always been cropped close to his skin. Dark bags puffed under his eyes, and the mole on his left cheek seemed bigger than ever on his wrinkled face. "What are you doing here?" he boomed. "At this hour? . . . Do you not know you have woken us up?" I bowed. "I am sorry, Grandfather." "Look at you," he hissed. "Your uniform is messy." The top two buttons of my uniform lay unbuttoned and my pants sagged. "Yes. You are right. But I have traveled far today. That is why I am here." "And that is what you always say, 'You are right,' but you do not believe your words. You do not change your ways. Are you so sure you are better than me and everyone else?" "I have never thought that." I prostrated myself again. "Then why are you here? Certainly you have no orders to come to this house while the war is becoming worse and worse. Certainly your commanding officer did not send you here. Are you so much smarter than him? Do you think you can shame me, that you can dishonor the favor which I have given you? That you can do whatever you want? That you can visit your family while others die?" "I have thought nothing of the sort." I bowed deeply. "Hush," my mother said, and she grabbed me, holding me tight. She ran her fingers through my hair. My aunt ran to the back room where the rice and vegetables were stored. "Come outside," my grandfather barked. "No. Leave him alone. Please," my mother rushed up to him. "He has never done anything but try to serve you. He will only stay until morning. It is not his fault that you are angry. Please. Go back to bed." "Then whose fault is it?" my grandfather demanded. "Whose is it?" "Your son's," my mother replied. She spoke of my father, her husband. My cousins, uncles and aunts stirred awake upstairs. The roof beams creaked. "No. I will not be shamed twice. Come with me." My grandfather pulled me outside by the neck. I did not struggle. Matsubara stood at attention as my grandfather walked out of the house. And that was when I realized he knew my grandfather's former rank, that he knew my grandfather had been a great general during the war with Russia, that my grandfather had led his men to victory through the scissors of night, through the passion and heat of war at the Battle of Mukden. My neck felt hot. My grandfather gripped me hard. Many times when I was a child, I had seen him slice a bale of hay with a sword in one stroke. Cold air pressed against my burning skin. I stumbled, bent over, my ears filled with the rustling of clothes and heavy footsteps, my cheek grazed by my grandfather's fist, the black of night blinding me. My cousin, Sachiko, wailed behind me, and an exchange of frantic questions was thrust at my mother. My whole family trailed behind me. My grandfather dragged me to the shed behind the house and pushed me through the door into the pottery studio. My leg hit one of the potting wheels and I fell over. "Bring a light," my grandfather ordered Matsubara. Matsubara complied, and I stood up, but I did not try to escape. My family waited outside the studio, unable to pierce my grandfather's territory, huddled around the door. "You owe your life to me, and I receive reports that you are lazy!" my grandfather shouted. "I have heard news from Mizuoshi-san's superiors that you are incapable of leading. Perhaps you would like to try fighting in China. Or in Singapore. Perhaps you would like to die with the others. Do you not realize you are alive because of me? Do you wish to shame me like your father?" The light from the lantern crept across the room, illuminating shelves and tables covered with pottery, the work of my father. The air smelled of clay. Gray and red washes of earth smeared the walls. Straw littered the floor. My father was in Sapporo designing ships on orders from the military, but his tea-ceremony bowls, vases, pots, pitchers and plates—each glazed in soft, swirling greens, yellows and blacks—remained as his legacy. "Do you wish to be a pacifist like your father? To cast away your honor? To end up in a tiny shack like this one with cold wind gnawing at your feet. How ignorant your father is! Playing peasant. How naive." A bamboo stick hung in the corner of the shed and my grandfather grabbed it. He beat a shelf of bowls. They shattered, tumbling against the dirt floor. He struck a large pot and it collapsed inward. "No," I begged. "Please. Do not." I slumped, weary, ashamed. "I am not like him, and you know it. I am not a pacifist. I have not been lazy. It is the false reports of Mizuoshi-san." My grandfather marched up to me and beat the bamboo against my leg and I crouched to the floor. "You see! You do not believe in your superiors. You say they lie. But even if they do, you must think they do not. You must accept it if they say black is white, if they say water is air. Only then will you be a good soldier. Only when you submit." My grandfather hit my back. "I could not cane you when your father was here. But now I will show you. Remove your shirt." "No!" my mother shouted. My aunt said the same. I limped up, barely able to stand, and fumbled with my shirt and my undershirt. I gave them to Matsubara, who stood in the corner with his back rigid, his eyes trying not to look at mine, but he did not interfere any more than a statue or a coat hanger receiving my clothing. "Against the wall," my grandfather yelled. "No! No more," my mother begged. She was near. She ran into the shack and grabbed my grandfather's arm. He threw her down. "Go away foolish woman." I braced myself against the wall. I did not resist. My grandfather beat me again and again, the bamboo hit my upper back, it pressed against my soft muscles. He was right and wrong: I did not deserve my rank or my life of relative safety, but I had worked tirelessly to please Mizuoshi-san. The cane beat into my skin until I bled. "Now go! And do not shame me again," he said. He put the cane neatly and carefully into the corner at last. I heaved, nearly vomiting. He straightened his kimono and walked back to the house slowly. My family parted for him to leave. My mother sent my cousin to get some water, then she washed my wounds. She revived me and wiped my skin with a wet cotton cloth, mixed with soap and with tears. She rocked me back and forth, running her fingers gently through my hair, kissing my forehead while my aunt and cousins watched in silence. And then in the darkness, in the night so black, much later, lying against the seat of the jeep, I returned to the Nijo palace with Matsubara.

Believe me when I say I did not try to discover more about the Kobe bomb the next few weeks. I concentrated only on my assigned work. The wounds from my grandfather burned, and I followed nothing but the orders of Mizuoshi-san. (Even he must have been satisfied with the diligence which I displayed, though he showed no signs of pleasure. On the contrary, he spent less and less time with me. In the morning, he no longer had me give him the intelligence report. This, I think, was not because he feared I had dis-obeyed him by going to Kobe—for he continued to insist I stay up each night when the transmissions were sent— but only because he wanted less contact with me.) Despite my problems with Mizuoshi-san, I would have let myself forget the Kobe bomb. I would have buried myself in my new routine and hid from him had there not been a second, a third, and then a fourth giant explosion.

And yet there was a second, a third, and then a fourth. The second in Wakayama on the eighteenth of June, the third in Yokkaichi on the fifth of July, the fourth in Maizuru on the twelfth. The explosion in Wakayama pulverized a secondary armaments factory. The bomb in Yokkaichi obliterated a port facility and a battleship. The attack on Maizuru was, perhaps, the most spectacular. The entire western switching yard for north/south trains twisted into snake-curved rails. It was not only the continuation of the bombs but the choice of targets which interested me immediately again, and I was unable to resist focusing my attention on the mystery of the bombs.

Without a doubt the targets were unusual, I thought, as I lay awake staring at my undecorated walls each night. The city of Wakayama had already been largely destroyed and the armaments factory was of little relevance there. The battleship in Yokkaichi was an old vessel, and the port was the least important of ten or more on Honshu, and although the switching yard in Maizuru was of note, there were at least two others to the east of greater significance. Why then had the bombs been dropped in these places if there were so few of them to be released? I fidgeted beneath my thin cotton sheet, unable to sleep. Thousands of regular bombs were falling on more significant targets every day. The objectives seemed odd, unlikely to instill fear into us or to cripple us; for surely the enemy must have known it would take an intelligence officer looking for reports of the bombs to find them.

Naturally, whenever I passed Mizuoshi-san, I did not know whether I should tell him of the new developments.

29

But if I did not he would find out sooner or later, and then he would punish me. Moreover, it was my duty to report everything to him. On the fifteenth of July, then, I approached him after I had spoken to each of the sources at the sites twice to confirm their reports.

"What should we do?" I asked Mizuoshi-san after giving him my report. We sat in his office. The battle of Okinawa had ended only twelve days before. (More than a hundred thousand of our men were dead, and the enemy was preparing an amphibious landing on the southern tip of Kyushu.) Sweat stains circled Mizuoshi-san's collar frequently during those days, as at that moment. "Nothing," he said. He sat across from me in his green padded chair, but he did not look at me. The window shutters were closed, leaving no more than a faint light, as if in a tomb. Mizuoshi-san seemed to be thinking of something else, perhaps of the morning report which detailed a strong counteroffensive in Manchuria. For a moment he glanced at me, coming back into focus. "There is nothing to do but wait," he said. "We do not see a significant pattern, and we are not even certain a single bomb has caused the damage." "But sir," I said. He raised his hand and I fell silent. The wrinkles across his forehead seemed to have deepened the last few weeks. "Tell Tanaka there will be no reports of the bombs. I will not tolerate any loss of determination on the part of the citizens." I scribbled his orders in my black notebook. "But sir—" "No one is to know of the bombs in the outpost either. Is that clear? I want no wild rumors or speculation affecting the efficiency of my troops." "But sir," I repeated, "Takayama and Hideoki know of the bombs already. They have seen the reports as they came in." "Then tell them to be quiet, too. Anyone caught mentioning the bombs will be placed in confinement, and I will hang any rumormonger if I hear word of the explosions outside of the palace." My legs stuck to my chair, and I wondered if Mizuoshi-san could see the sweat on my uniform. It was unbearably hot and muggy despite the shutters. "But it may be too late to stem any rumors," I said. "The sources at each of the sites are discussing the explosions already." "Then order them to be quiet, too. Do I have to explain everything to you? I want no mention of the bombs. Anywhere." Mizuoshi-san jerked up from his chair and wiped his face with a handkerchief. "The people will not believe the rumors if the explosion is unacknowledged in the papers." "But sir, the bomb *does* exist," I nearly shouted, "we must tell Tokyo." Mizuoshi-san laughed, placing his face close to mine. "Do you wish to disobey me? Do you really wish to erode the indifference which I have cultivated toward you the last few weeks? I have seen you trying to please me, you know. Yes. Your efforts have not gone unnoticed. They even amuse me at times, as long as I do not have to think about you much. But you will bring my anger back." I pulled my shoulders up, correcting my slightly slouched position. I had never been good at maintaining the stiff posture required of an officer. "But sir! I do not wish to disobey you at all." "Then speak to me no more of this." Mizuoshi-san circled me and he walked to the other end of the room. "I was only saying," I whispered to myself—air whistled through my lips so faintly it seemed an invisible puff—"that we must tell Tokyo." Mizuoshi-san bent toward me. "What?" "Nothing. I am sorry sir." I bowed. "I was only speaking to myself." Mizuoshi-san struck his fist against the wall; dust darted, lit by a slit of light through the shutters. "And you were saying something about how we should inform Tokyo. Do you think I am deaf because I am older? Do you think I have no reason to keep this information from Tokyo?" He rushed behind me and bent his head over my shoulder to speak loudly into my ear. "I have every reason not to inform them. We have no idea where the next bomb will hit. We have no idea why the existing targets have been chosen. We have no information why the bomb is used so infrequently. We have no indication the bomb is more threatening than any other weapon the enemy possesses when they use them together. Do you wish to anger General Hashimoto after the battle of Okinawa? While the war is tumbling in on us? Do you wish for me to say, 'General Hashimoto, I have discovered a bomb of insignificance to the war. My second officer says you must be informed of it. There are other battles of more significance, I know, but you must be made aware of a giant bomb which the enemy does not use much.' Is this what you want me to say?" I desired to shake my head yes, to nod, but I held myself straight as Mizuoshi-san pressed his lips close to my ear. My legs pushed tightly against the front of my chair, and I sat stiffly. But I wanted to tell Mizuoshi-san that surely Tokyo would hear of the bombs eventually and that then they would become angry in any case. I wanted to tell him that *all* information is good if it is true and that all intelligence must be known. I wanted to tell him that precious time was being lost while we waited for rumor to reach its twisted fingers to Tokyo, and that the first rule of intelligence, which even he had taught me, was never to hide anything, for knowing the truth only makes an army stronger. Veracity is the mirror from which to fight back, the image necessary to find and to heal an army's wound. I wanted to tell him that the bomb *was* significant, that it was huge, that it would destroy us if used in numbers as great as the regular bombs. (All he needed to do was to use his imagination to see the consequences.) Yes, all of these things I wanted to tell him. But I said nothing. Mizuoshi-san had long since forgotten his own rules. He tapped his ragged fingernails against the hardwood of my armrest as he bent over me. He had fallen into the habit of biting his nails recently. He pulled away from me and paced the room. "I will hold you responsible for any news leaked," he said. I jumped up and held myself at attention. "The rumor will not leave this office," I said and I bowed, then I bowed again. And then I rushed out of the room to tell Tanaka to halt any news of the bombs.

But as I strode through the palace, past the central chamber where the great Shogun Ieyasu had met with his samurais to hand down his wise and careful decisions, I was already thinking about the puzzle of the bombs, trying to put the pieces together. For only one thought coursed through me. What was the enemy's plan?

On the nineteenth of July I walked to the golden temple to see my best friend Naoki. Throughout my childhood Naoki had been my closest companion. Every day we came home from school together, stopping frequently to buy ice cream at Yamanashi's or to tease a girl named Yukiko, and on most days we combed the cedar hills above my house looking for trees to climb or for toads. When we were older we did our homework together—painting, calligraphy or writing haikus—and we became drunk for the first time at the age of fourteen with a liter of sake which Naoki had stolen from his father. But although we spent most of our time together, Naoki left me to join the Shinjo monastery in Obama when he was seventeen. Six months before the victory at Pearl Harbor he departed for the southern tip of Fukui prefecture, seventy kilometers to the north. (This, it seemed, was a lucky decision, as if Naoki had sensed the battle with China was going to expand, that it was going to get worse, for only monks were exempt from conscription.) A week before I went to see Naoki in Kyoto, he had been transferred to the golden temple because of attacks on the port of Obama. He sent word to me as soon as he arrived in Kyoto. Naturally, I went to see him the first opportunity I had. On the nineteenth, I was given the day off, as was Matsubara, and we went together. Four months had passed since our last break, and Mizuoshi-san had shown no intention of granting another respite, but he had finally relented after one of the soldiers, Shigata, a fairly docile intelligence operator, had thrown his fist through a window in a minor dispute over food. After dinner that night, before going to bed, the voice of a soldier had pierced the thin walls of my room, "Do you think we will surrender?" It was the first time I had heard such open speculation, and I knew I wanted the Emperor to relent, too, but the thought was unthinkable.

As we walked to the temple the streets were filled with red and white flags. Naoki had told me in a second letter to meet him at three o'clock and not before. It was two, so we ambled. There was still street-life in Kyoto even during the last days of the war. (The city, as I have mentioned to you before, was relatively safe. Minor damage to an outer building of the Old Imperial Palace was the only significant harm, and this, it was commonly understood amongst us in the intelligence community, was the result of a stray bomb dropped during cloudy weather when the enemy, no doubt, was unable to see their proper target. Only ninety-seven people died, thankfully, from air attacks in Kyoto during the war.)

Before we arrived at the temple, Matsubara and I meandered through the old Sembon district. The stores were empty of goods but customers went into them in any case, and so did we. The people seemed to need to talk to the owners, to speculate about the next battle or to condemn the hot weather, and occasionally a half cigarette could be found. Back outside, a large crowd gathered at a street corner to place bets on a portable roulette wheel—though gambling was illegal—and at another to watch kabuki. A giant white horse, performed by two men, rolled in wild acrobatics until the horse threw its rider, a man dressed like

Uncle Sam, to the ground. The crowd watched intently and laughed, as did I, though I realized the enemy was not nearly so stupid. Further up the street two men with crutches plodded through the main thoroughfare, their legs wrapped in casts, their arms and foreheads bandaged, and I shuddered to look at them. The pedestrians were packed so tightly it was difficult to see to the end of each block and many bumped into the injured soldiers. Tattered bags and wooden chests barricaded the sidewalks. Relatives continued to flood into the city each day from more devastated towns. "Hot noodles!" a young boy shouted. "Hot noodles!" There was a good deal of money to make in the luxury of selling soba at the time. A beggar reached in front of the boy to sneak a bowl, but the boy stayed near his wooden pot, beating away the mendicant, hiding his coins. The beggar had only one eye and an empty dry red socket in the space of the other. His legs were deformed and he moved by swinging himself forward on his arms. For a moment I looked at him. I wanted to buy him a bowl of noodles but I had no money, then I wanted to grab him a bowl but I was afraid of starting a commotion. (For who knew what the police would do if they caught me? At the very least they would report me to Mizuoshi-san and sully the name of our unit, and then everyone would be punished. Theft was prosecuted mercilessly at the time.) I grabbed Matsubara and pulled him forward, trying not to look at the beggar. But I could not help turning back. The beggar was tapping the leg of the noodle boy with his dirty fingers, crying wordlessly. A man dressed in a fine deep brown kimono passed me and I bowed to him. "But sir," I said, "most honorable sir, do you not have a coin to give this beggar?" The man stopped and looked at me, startled. A small cluster of people halted at my words, and the beggar turned from the leg of the noodle boy to look at the wealthy man. Everyone waited to see what would happen next. The wealthy man looked at me coldly, like a devil spirit in a giant painting, glowering down at a mortal from the heavens. He stared at me for over a minute without moving. But then, in one quick motion he pulled a half-yen coin from his kimono and dropped it to the ground. "If he wants to, he can take it," he said. The beggar did not move, he huddled far away. I stooped to pick up the coin to give it to him. But before I could reach the money he leaped, lunging his body forward, plunging his face into the dirty street, snatching and grabbing for the coin with his outstretched hand. I tried to right him quickly, but he pushed me away. He raised his thin body and spat at my leg. He cursed me wordlessly, gesturing that I could not steal his coin. And filled with the shame that I had caused him to grovel, that I had made him reveal just how weak he was—wishing that I had not stopped to look at him in the first place—I clutched Matsubara and hurried toward the temple of the golden pavilion. The temple was far from the Nijo palace. We still had a kilometer to go. It was almost three. And without a doubt I did not want to walk the streets of Kyoto anymore.

A few minutes later we arrived at the temple. If you have ever had the chance to see the golden pavilion the way I did that day, then surely you are lucky. The temple is filled with tourists now, clicking cameras at the placid pool of lilies, zooming their telephoto lenses across the water at the majestic three-tiered pavilion. The tourists fail to ever stop to see the true beauty, the silence of the moment. But the monastery was closed to tourists at the time. (And this was why I had brought Matsubara with me, although he did not know Naoki. For I knew he would never see the temple if I did not bring him.) Near the northwest edge of town we hurried along the foothills of the city, through the outer temple park full of pines, toward the ancient wooden door to the thick walls which surround the monastery. As we approached the temple, I passed the tame deer foraging in the park almost without seeing them, I was still thinking so much about the beggar. (Had I been wrong to help him? Wrong to beg for him when he was already begging for himself? Wrong to make the wealthy man pay what I myself did not pay? I wanted Naoki to tell me.) Naoki opened the door immediately when I knocked. He threw his hand over my mouth and hugged me. I attempted to speak, but he silenced me again. He led us through a long open corridor, up a flight of stone steps, through another corridor, and then into the main garden. He placed us on a wide bed of moss and pointed us toward the central pond. "But why the silence?" I finally blurted out. Naoki pointed for me to look at the lake, at the pavilion, but I could not help studying him first. Four years had passed since the last time I had seen him, and he had shaved his hair evenly—a surprise since he never combed it before. Still, I noticed a small patch, a small clump of hair a little longer, which anyone else would have thought was a mistake were it not on the head of Naoki. His long, thin face was still smooth and young. His dark brown eyes darted over Matsubara and me, and he grinned as if guarding a secret. He had a chestnut-colored monk's robe on, and his ears stood out more than usual due to the shortness of his hair, but he still looked scrappily handsome. "Look," he finally whispered, and he pointed emphatically. I followed his fingers to the pond, then to the pavilion. And there the pavilion was: its three curved roofs lilted softly upwards at the far end of the pond, one level floating above the next. The windows were carved with metal filigree. A phoenix statue of gold crowned the top of the tea-house and the third level was gilded completely with gold, shining as brightly as a needle in the sun. The front of the pavilion hovered over the pond on stilts, like a ship of jewels safely harbored. An island of green weathered rock and small sculpted pines rose from the center of the pond, as if in echo of the beauty of the pavilion. Clusters of smaller lichen-covered rocks peeked from the water, orbiting the central island like planets around the sun. For more than a minute, I breathed deeply and I listened to the sound of birds calling from one fragrant cedar tree to another. Blue sky reflected in the water. White silk clouds floated across the mirrored glass of liquid. Thick beds of moss surrounded the pond. "It's beautiful," I said to Naoki. He put his finger to his lips again. "But why the complete silence?" I asked once more. "Because that is what the temple *is*." Naoki closed his eyes and listened. "The beauty of the temple is simply meant to overwhelm the viewer so that they will be quiet for a moment. I wanted you to see the temple as it is." He leaned toward me, pausing for his words to sink in. "And because I'm supposed to be praying now too," he said a little louder, then he laughed loudly. "Everyone is in the main hall for the three o'clock prayer. But I've skipped it to see you . . . You're not supposed to be here either, you know. No visitors allowed. The head priest will beat us mercilessly if he finds us. But then he would have to be skipping the three o'clock prayer, too, wouldn't he?" Naoki grinned devilishly. He stood up, ducked his head, and ran a little around the pond, then motioned us forward. He searched for any suspecting monks in the buildings at the far end of the garden, and we followed him, running around the pond to the pavilion tea-house. "I'll tell them I was sick," he whispered as we reached the pavilion. He glanced at his watch. "We still have another hour before the prayer is over. Go ahead. Go inside, quick . . . The pavilion is the most forbidden place for anyone except the head priest. He'll never come looking for us in here." I looked at Naoki suspiciously. "But what if we're caught? Why didn't you tell me visitors are forbidden? We could have met somewhere else." "Because then I wouldn't have seen you until I had permission to leave. And sometimes I'm told that takes two months. Just go inside!" Naoki pushed me onto the balcony of the pavilion over the water. The railings of the terrace were covered with gold. The tea-house was built by the great lord Yoshimitsu, grandson of the emperor Ashikaga Takuji, more than six hundred years before. The wood on the balcony was so smooth I was ashamed to step on it. "Hurry up!" Naoki hissed and he scurried forward, but I remained paralyzed until he slid the door to the pavilion open. "Put your shoes in your pockets and carry them," he ordered. "Leave nothing outside or someone will notice them." "But I'm still not sure I want to *go* inside," I said. "Of course you do." Naoki pulled off one of my shoes and gave it to me to put into my pocket, "That's what you always used to say when we were younger whenever we did something risky. But then you were always happy to have followed, weren't you?" Matsubara removed his shoes and placed them inside the pockets of his baggy military pants. The two of them waited for me. I hesitated, but I could not resist. "That's the problem with you," Naoki said as he closed the sliding door to the pavilion. (The fine paintings of mountains on the screen were so delicate I stepped away from them. Ancient scrolls and vases, fresh flowers and new sticks of incense lined the walls of the first floor. We climbed a steep wooden ladder to the second floor.) "You always hesitate at the last minute," Naoki continued. "You start something with great certainty and then you lose your will." (The second floor was even more delicate than the first. The windows were smaller and the ornaments were fewer, but the quality of the paintings was even higher if possible.) "Perhaps I should stay here," Matsubara suggested, "to warn if anyone is coming." I couldn't tell what difference it would make if someone warned us or not by the time we were on the second floor. There was nowhere to hide. The rooms

41

were sparsely decorated, without closets. But Matsubara wanted to give us a chance to be alone, I think, and he stayed below as we climbed another ladder to the third floor. "You're right," I said to Naoki as we neared the top. "I *do* lose my will." I felt nervous just entering the third level. "On our way here, for example, we met a beggar in Sembon. I wanted to buy him a bowl of noodles but I didn't have any money. So I asked a wealthy man to help, but he didn't want to support the beggar. He just dropped a measly half-yen coin on the ground to shame him." "And?" Naoki prodded me. We were standing at the top, around the opening where the ladder poked through the floor. "And. So. When the wealthy man dropped the coin on the ground, it was far from the beggar, so I tried to pick it up for him. But the beggar thought I was stealing his coin, so he spat on me. And that made me think. Perhaps I shouldn't have tried to help him in the first place because he was capable of helping himself. Or perhaps I shouldn't have asked the wealthy man for money because I didn't give the beggar any myself." I waited for Naoki to reply. "That's ridiculous," he said. "You see!" He threw his hands into the air. "Why should you doubt you are right when your intentions are good? How could you have known the beggar was going to be crazy when you decided to help him? Or how can you give money to someone if you don't have any with you? You think too much. You always look for two sides to every problem. But sometimes there is only one of merit. If you know a thing inside, you should have more conviction. What's wrong with two friends meeting up here for example? Come on. I'll make you some tea. I hear there's good tea up here." Naoki led me to the center of the room, and I remembered a lecture my father had given me about conviction when I was fifteen. He had said there was pig-headedness, like my grandfather's, which was meant only to support a person's will, and conviction, the fight for justice no matter how small or large. My father had said he was a potter of conviction, free from the military or from any other constraint. His words came to me now like a pungent smell. "So how is your family?" Naoki asked. He sat on the floor. The weave of the mats looked so tight it could have held water. The room felt incredibly light, as if it were a floating balloon, or a bungalow flying. Sunlight burst through the windows into every corner. The ceiling of cedar hovered like a parasol, feathered with gold outside. The outline of the water garden lay like a colorful painting below. Naoki searched for utensils for the tea ceremony. It was hard to believe a place so quiet and beautiful could exist during the war. "My father hasn't sent a letter in a while," I told him. "But I imagine he is waiting for the war to end. He said in his last letter that the shipyard in Hokkaido is like a prison. He said he only wants to get back to his pottery." Naoki nodded. "Sort of the way I considered the monastery in Obama. And now maybe here, too. But it's the only way out." He discovered a bowl for tea at last, a bamboo teaspoon and a small bamboo whisk, a cloth and some green tea. He lit a few pieces of charcoal in the ceremonial cooking pit. "But you know," I said faintly, "I believed in the war at the beginning." I stared out the windows at the garden. Naoki blew on the charcoal, concentrating on it until it began to glow. He didn't respond. "I don't know what my father will think of me when he comes home. He always wanted me to go with you to the monastery, you know." "Yes. I know," Naoki said. "It was only because of his pleading to Grandfather that I was given the job in the intelligence command post." "I know that, too," Naoki said. (And how can I explain the silence which followed? The silence so strong even the sunlight seemed to make noise.) Naoki ladled water from an ancient porcelain Chinese pot. He filled a copper kettle then he placed the pot over the flames and let the water boil. He cleaned the tea bowl. My father had taught us the tea ceremony when we were children. Naoki performed the ceremony spontaneously, moving gracefully at any moment as he wished, adding any gesture, as my father did; but I followed the rules strictly as the Urasenke tradition proscribed. He placed green tea gently at the bottom of the bowl. He added water and let the sound of the liquid rise like a blooming flower. He grasped the bamboo whisk firmly and swirled the tea, flicking his wrist back and forth like a flowing ribbon until the tea was perfectly frothed. He placed the whisk to one side, bowed, and offered me the tea. I raised the bowl to him first, drank slowly, and tasted every drop, then I looked at the bowl and its beauty as required. I returned the bowl, and Naoki took it to clean ceremoniously. I looked out the windows at the garden as Naoki cleaned the bowl. My eyes glazed as I thought about my father, and it was only gradually that the central island of the pond commanded my attention. The island stood out like a capitol in the midst of provincial towns. The tinier rocks peeked through the water, paying homage to the center. The design mesmerized me, and I stared at it until I almost no longer saw the rocks. At the end of the ceremony, I spoke to Naoki at last. "Yes. I think my father always preferred you," I said almost to myself. I looked outside at the splash of color in the water garden. The colors seemed a wash now, an oblivion. The room was silent, too silent. But in a few minutes I saw the garden clearly once again. The central island seemed to leap up at me, a beacon. The rocks appeared like a map, as if the design had burned itself into my mind from when I'd stared at it before. And suddenly, I saw the smaller islands as if they were equidistant from the center, forming a circle. The asymmetry had diverted my attention from the true pattern before, as the asymmetry of the four bombs surrounding Kyoto obscured their true meaning. But as clearly as the rocks ran around the central island, pointing toward it, the Kobe-type bombs ran around Kyoto. Kyoto was the target. It would be the final target. "I must go," I said to Naoki, and I jumped up. "I must leave." "What's wrong?" he demanded. He flinched. "It has nothing to do with you. I promise. But I must go. I have discovered something very important." My whole body shook with energy. "Something extremely important." I rushed to the ladder, and Naoki did not try to stop me. He only ran after me and touched my shoulder as I left. "I'll write to you soon," he yelled as I scurried down the ladder. I grabbed Matsubara on the way. And armed with my new knowledge I ran quickly from the pavilion. For I knew I had to pursue the mystery of the bombs with all of my soul.

I remember sixteen more bombs dropped during the last week of July. The targets remain with me as clearly as the moles and wrinkles, the indentations and lines on my face. This morning I studied myself before sitting down to write to you again, and as I looked at myself in the mirror I wondered: would I look different if I had made another decision fifty years ago? Certainly I would have more hair on my head. Fewer wrinkles under my eyes. Whatever success I may have had since the war—my grandchildren, my wife— I cannot right my old wrong.

This morning, I thought about your grandfather, too. The newspapers report he was a successful man.

When I arrived at the Nijo palace from the golden temple, I ran to my room to find the colored map where I had plotted the bombing targets. I kept the map beneath my toiletries in the hope that Mizuoshi-san would never inspect there. The four targets circled Kyoto clearly. But why? What was the enemy waiting for to attack our old capital? Could it be that the bombs were only hints to encourage us to surrender, a warning to our generals of an impending escalation of the war, a final hint before the enemy killed so many in Kyoto that the wrath of our population, they knew, would turn stronger against them? But the enemy had never shown such subtlety before. Three quarters of Tokyo burned in one night. Yokohama, Kobe and Osaka had been completely destroyed. Iwo Jima and Okinawa. I did not believe our city had been spared to assist American propaganda, to cultivate good will toward the Americans, as our senior officers concluded.

Then perhaps the rumors in the streets were true. Perhaps Kyoto *was* too ancient and beautiful a city to be demolished. Perhaps it *was* protected by the Emperor's spirit. But I had read of the furnaces of Dresden and Berlin and seen pictures in the newspaper of masterpiece churches destroyed, and how many sacred temples had been burned in our own country? Then perhaps the enemy did not have enough of the bombs. Perhaps they could not produce them in large quantities. But even a few well-chosen targets in Kyoto would have destroyed more important factories than the targets which had already been demolished. (And here my thoughts leapt, as surely they must with all moments of swift insight, though I have had only a few. For suddenly it seemed to me it was precisely the invaluableness of Kyoto which had spared the city.) For how does a hunter trap his prey? By luring it with meat and delicacies, with salt and young bamboo. To catch carp, place rice cakes inside a net. To catch crab, stuff fish inside a cage. Kyoto was sweet and alluring, ripe with safety, filling with more and more factories every day, plump with refugees pressing out more bullets and bombs, airplanes and guns, gorged with the illusion of safety, unprepared to fight. Like ants called to a pot of honey, we had arrived, only to be trapped in the funeral pyre which would be Kyoto. It seemed so clear to me as I looked at the map, and then even clearer that only three other big cities remained, mysteriously, unbombed. Yet despite this feeling I did not tell Mizuoshi-san of my theory until he demanded it of me in August.

In the meantime, I watched sixteen more of the Kobe-type bombs fall. At night in the decoding room I requested reports from other intelligence command posts. I had not thought to look around the rest of the country before, where other bombs might have been dropped, because I had not wanted to anger Mizuoshi-san or to spread rumors. But now I gathered my clues. I wired only officers whom I knew. I waited until the few other night operators in our headquarters were busy with other tasks, then I teletyped a single command post at a time. "The superior officer, 09B, requests reports of all bombing in your area. Respond to second officer." Replies came back immediately. It was common to share such information. (Only reports of unusual activities could not be sent to other stations without high level approval to contain the spread of disinformation and panic. Tokyo alone knew all, but I discovered what I needed.)

And without a doubt, the reports discouraged me at first. There *was* no news of the giant bombs, no Kyoto pattern, not even a hint of more explosions around our old capital. For six days I waited until the first of the sixteen bombs dropped on the 27th of July in Koriyama. The second through fifth fell on the 28th, the six through ninth on the 29th, the tenth through twelfth on the 30th, and the rest on the last day of July. Three bombs exploded within a hundred and twenty kilometers of Niigata: the seaport remained our last giant western harbor; almost all shipping to China passed through the port. Four bombs dropped within a hundred and fifty kilometers of Hiroshima, the closest at Niihama. The city served as our central embarkation point for the army to the south, the harbor serviced the navy as an assembly plant, the heavy industry there endured unbombed. The last of the giant explosions surrounded Nagasaki and the arsenal at Kokura, our largest munitions plant on Honshu. Both targets remained as untouched as the huge primordial pine forests of Hokkaido.

As I studied the reports, I nearly leapt from my chair with the horror of darkness premonitioned, with the excitement of unwanted insight. The cities of the sixteen targets had already been attacked, and each was relatively insignificant, as with the first four explosions. But despite my agitation I said nothing out of the ordinary to the other operators. "Good night," I told them each morning at four o'clock, "You may go." The three of them bowed sloppily, half asleep, and then they left. I, too, had bags under my eyes. Regular reports had expanded as the enemy increased the ferocious fury of their activity.

With the others gone, I sat alone in the large decoding room, surrounded by empty metal desks. The teletypers and radios fell silent at last. The room was as quiet as the inside of a nut. The dim incandescent lights hung stiffly from their thick black cables. (Electricity was spotty. We relied on our own generator, but oil was scarce.) The air was heaviest and most humid at that time before dawn. From the first of the sixteen bombs until the last, I remained in the decoding room each night until the sun rose, plotting the explosions on my map. I traced circles, using a compass, trying to connect the dots around each final target. But the twenty bomb sites never quite perfectly fitted. And perhaps it was this fact, this single fact alone—added to much more important circumstances—which halted me whenever I began to radio Tokyo, and which must have prevented Tokyo from figuring out everything on their own.

On my fourth and final attempt to contact Tokyo, I sat rigidly before the transmitter at five in the morning; there was always someone awake to receive a message in Tokyo. The radio looked so prepared, so ready to send my message. I adjusted the frequency to match the receiver in Tokyo. I put on my headset and inched the large microphone in front of me. I cleared my throat and wiped my palms on my pants, then brushed my lips with my handkerchief. I turned the radio on with a slow motion and practiced my speech. "Captain Murayama Kazuo, second officer, 09B, reporting sir. Request permission to give full report. Unusual bombing has been noted in the area." I clutched the map in front of me with the four final targets circled and stared at the targets, each imperfectly ringed by the giant bombs, yet each clearly surrounded. But before I could send the beginning code to indicate a forthcoming transmission, I turned the radio off. Thoughts of my grandfather filled my mind. It was the fourth time I had extinguished the transmitter at a similar moment, and I sat weary, my brain a whirl. For what did my grandfather matter to me? What could he possibly matter compared to my father? And yet, his image crept into my mind, a vision of him dressed in his dark gray kimono, his short gray hair, his almost bald head, his long black-lacquered sword swinging by his side, his shoulders square, his eyes piercing. He spoke to me in his booming voice. "You! You have dishonored me. *Me.* The one who saved your life. *Me.* Because of a foolish dream . . . What significance does that pattern of rocks have? None. And for this you have shamed me. Out of arrogance. Because you believe you know more than your commanding officer . . . Who knows more than their commanding officer? No one. If I could, I would whip you again now: Twice. Three times. Four." I covered my ears but I could not muffle my grandfather's voice. "You! You cannot escape me. Who do you think your father and Naoki are? Traitors. Disgraces to their families . . . Your father is unfit to be an eldest son. How can you shame me? *Me,* the one who saved your life. You, the next eldest son." I threw my headset on its stand and ran from the radio. I could not rid myself of my grandfather's voice. I dropped the map as I ran out the door and scurried through the palace from one room to another, from one chamber to the next, until I slumped at last on the outer wooden walkway which surrounded the castle. I lay with my back against the palace wall, with my knees pressed against my head, tears soaking through my cotton pants onto my thighs. And why was it the same each day? Why, when I was so sure of myself? When I thought I was so sure. For four days now. When there was no time to waste. Hot currents of pain swam through my head. The tiny moon, a sliver, was setting behind the black pattern of pines in the palace garden; the white slice blurred behind my tears. The sky changed to dark blue. The sun would rise soon. For more than an hour I huddled in a ball, waiting until the sun would rise, until a flicker of energy would enter my body . . . I must, I thought. I must get up. I must go back before I lose my will. Mizuoshi-san will come to the main office in an hour, and then another day will be lost . . . I watched the sun until it climbed a hand above the ground, floating like an orange rose, until the sunlight hit me and I lifted my weary body. I stole quietly back to the decoding room. The floorboards of the outer walkway supported me firmly. The whole palace loomed. The dark porcelain-tiled roof of the palace looked silhouetted, curving downward in a gentle arc in the morning light, like the wing of a great crane in flight, as if the palace were ready to lift me. I hurried into the decoding room, to where dapples of orange light splayed across the walls, mixing with shadows, creating a confusing pattern, and wended my way to the radio. I put on my headset and turned on the radio and adjusted the microphone. I practiced my speech and prepared to transmit the beginning code. I focused all of my energy on my task and looked at nothing but the microphone in front of me as if in a trance. "But what are you doing?" a voice suddenly interrupted. "Go away!" I said to my grandfather. But the voice was higher than my grandfather's. It approached from the corner of the room. "Who are you speaking to?" it demanded, and I froze. "Could it be that you are calling Tokyo when I have told you not to?" Mizuoshi-san bounded up to me, and I bowed. He thrust my map in front of me and twisted me away from the radio and pressed his face into mine. "Yes! Who are you reporting to without having informed me?" He checked the frequency on the radio, then shook me and pinched my cheek. I tried to bow, but he lifted me by my hair. "Your silence reveals complicity. You are as untrustworthy as a pig." "It is true," I said, and I crouched to my knees. "But I have discovered the final targets of the giant bombs." I pressed my hands together and pleaded for mercy, begging Mizuoshi-san to listen. He struck me on the mouth. "Such stupid games. Chasing after ghosts. I have seen your crazy map. In the middle of the room, no less, with your name on it. You would not make a good spy even if your grandfather let you." "But I have discovered a trap!" I said. "They are going to destroy Kyoto. Do not listen to me if you do not want to. Do not think of me when I tell you what I am going to say. Think only of *what* I say. Think of the trap. The *traps*. We must evacuate Kyoto, Hiroshima, Nagasaki, and Niigata." Mizuoshi-san laughed. "The enemy bombs us everywhere," he shouted. "We have no defenses. All Japan is trapped. The enemy does not need a trap. What trap? You are speaking foolishly." "They are hunting us," I said. "The four bombs and the sixteen new bombs which I have plotted on the map are only practice. They are waiting for our cities to become filled before they destroy us. They are baiting us into the cities with safety before they massacre us." Mizuoshi-san pushed my head down harder, and I spoke quickly. I had seen him relent, but only when he could see a flicker of agreement immediately. "Then why does the enemy not wait elsewhere?'' Mizuoshi-san asked. ''Why do they not wait in Tokyo? Why do they not wait in Nagoya? Why do they not wait in Kobe? In Osaka? In Yokohama? In Fukuoka? In Chiba? In Kawasaki? I do not have time for your games. For your crazy plots. You should do necessary work. But instead you indulge yourself in childish pranks while others die.'' I bowed deeply. ''But sir,'' I said with my face near to the floor, ''What about the twenty bombs? Why have they been dropped?'' I waited for him to reply. I thought I had made him think. ''And why *have* they been dropped?'' Mizuoshi-san answered without waiting. ''What difference does it make? I do not know why the enemy wishes to use these bombs. I do not know why they use them in places where they are useless, and why they drop others where they are painful. But they do not wait to destroy.'' ''But sir, you have not seen the great power of the bombs. You have not seen what they can do. You have not witnessed what they will do to the final targets.'' ''And neither have you! How can you be so sure your reports are true?'' ''Because I have seen the bomb,'' I whispered. Mizuoshi-san raised my head by my chin. He pressed my cheek between his thumb and forefinger. ''You are dreaming. You are crazy,'' he said. ''You have lost all reason.'' ''I went to Kobe to see the bomb.'' ''When?'' ''When I was supposed to be in Osaka. After inspecting the reports of sabotage at the railway yard.'' Mizuoshi-san bent backward, puzzled. ''I saw the bomb.'' ''You? You disobeyed me?'' ''I saw the whole dock torn apart.'' ''You. You disobeyed my will?'' ''They will destroy all of Kyoto. All of the targets.''

Mizuoshi-san snatched me by the neck. "Then what would you have me do? What do you want me to tell Tokyo? That we must evacuate Niigata and Kyoto, Hiroshima and Nagasaki. That we must close the arsenal at Kokura? That we must move millions of people because a few giant bombs have exploded more than a hundred kilometers from these cities? . . . And where will you send all of these people? Where will you put them to be safe? You! You are too young! Too arrogant, Kazuo. Untested. Even a new born pig has more sense than you. Even the village idiot." Mizuoshi-san pushed me to the ground. He stood and wiped his pants, then hurried to the door. "Come here! Come," he shouted to one of the morning soldiers who had arrived to clean the floors. "Take him to the central courtyard and call everyone to see his sentencing." The soldier—Haruo— approached and lifted me gently from the floor. "No. Not that way. He has lost his rank. Do not show him any respect." Haruo gripped my arm. "You will see!" I shouted to Mizuoshi-san. "You will see that I am right." "Bind his hands. Tie them behind his back. Do not leave him alone," Mizuoshi-san ordered. "I have removed a young thorn from my paw," he exalted, and then he left.

And how did the soldiers stand that morning as I received my sentence? Straight, like rods of bamboo. I crouched on my knees, crumpled beneath the red and white flag in the center of the Nijo court. The fine white pebbles of the courtyard pressed against my flesh. I had been stripped naked except for a white loin-cloth, and I could not lift my head, but I could see forward when I tilted my eyes upward. The soldiers surrounded me, circumscribing the court. They held their arms behind their backs. They spread their legs apart until they formed a wall around me. At Mizuoshi-san's command a small soldier—a young boy, a new recruit whom I did not know—marched in front of me with a scroll to read my sentence. He bowed to Mizuoshi-san and then to the flag. "The former Captain Murayama Kazuo is hereby sentenced to imprisonment for insubordination, for acts committed against his superior officer and against the Emperor. Let this be a lesson to everyone . . ." Three soldiers carried me to a wooden cell at the back of the courtyard. The room was hot like a swamp. Black and green mold grew on the walls. And it was there, barely able to stand or to sit, accompanied by rats, that I remained for a month.

I do not know if you have seen Hiroshima. It is full of neon lights now. The citizens have resurrected the old trolley cars—painted them orange and green—and the bullet train comes into the station every hour, on the hour, when it is supposed to. The old palace, two hundred meters from the flash point of the bomb, rises majestically above the town, rebuilt. Ancient-looking wood covers the castle side walls, and the stones at the base of the structure lend a feeling of massive permanence. In the spring time, grandparents and grandchildren celebrate the new season, picnicking beneath the fresh cherry blossoms of the palace garden. I have been to Hiroshima many times to see the parents of my wife.

And yet, the city is the shell of a ghost now. The

maple trees which line the rivers tell all. They stand exactly the same height, placed in the ground at exactly the same time. You will not find an old tree in Hiroshima. Never a fat tree to catch your attention. Nor will you see an old building. The city must support the whole glass industry of Japan! There is nothing but new office buildings downtown, prosperous businesses, new cars, and the cleaned-up atomic bomb dome.

Yes, I have seen Hiroshima. In early October I went to the city, only a month after the end of the war. The Emperor surrendered on August 14th, of course. An American second lieutenant released me from my cell a few weeks later. (Matsubara had told me about the bomb already. He snuck by my cell to bring me extra food whenever he could. Three days after the first morning of my imprisonment he came to me with the news. "There has been a huge bomb dropped over Hiroshima!" he told me. "The radio does not tell much. They say it may be a new kind of bomb." I pressed my head hard against the door trying to hear. I sweated profusely; my heart constricted. "What kind of bomb?" I asked. "They do not say. But the whole city is destroyed." Matsubara paused suddenly. "I must go. Someone is coming." "Where is Mizuoshi-san?" I demanded. "I cannot say." Matsubara's voice ran away. "He is gone," I thought I heard him sputter, "locked inside his room." His voice left me. The soldier on duty shoved a bowl of half-cooked rice through my trap door. Each of the guards had orders not to communicate with me.)

I do not know what Mizuoshi-san did during those

three days after Hiroshima, perhaps he drank sake in his room until he passed out, but the second bomb dropped on Nagasaki on August 9th.

When I arrived in Hiroshima, I jumped off the truck which I had hitchhiked on. The sun burned hot, the sky was cloudless. The truck stopped a few kilometers outside of the city; American soldiers required a pass for any vehicle to enter, and I walked the rest of the way. The road turned quickly to dirt. The only remaining pavement clung around potholes, as if the depressions had given some form of mysterious protection. American military convoys zoomed past, filled with smiling soldiers. Their trucks kicked dust into the air and I covered my face. A steady flow of refugees lumbered along the road, walking in single file for the most part, carrying sacks of cloth filled with belongings or pushing carts, moving in both directions, but few volunteered to speak to me. "What did you see?" I asked whoever I could. "A white ball," an old man told me. "Nothing," a big man said. He had been blown on his back beneath a train. "A black cloud," a teenage boy muttered.

Over the years, I have discovered the meaning of the Kobe-type bombs. They were called the "Pumpkin Program," a small but important part of the Manhattan Project. The enemy tested their "dummy" bombs, shaped like pumpkins like the Fat Man, to see if their planes could carry heavy payloads. The uranium abomination dropped over Hiroshima weighed five thousand kilos. The enemy wanted our soldiers to become used to small groups of B-29s flying at high altitude as they conducted target practice.

By late morning, I arrived in the center of Hiroshima. The earth was red, everything was covered with dust. A howling wind blew across the flat city, gathering pieces of wood and flecks of glass into spiraling funnels. I had noticed a strange phenomenon on my way to the center. The plants were growing furiously, as if they had been given blood meal. They sprouted rabidly from the ground, poking through burnt corpses, skeletons and melted tiles. The radiation, I learned later, fed them. Outside the city, fall had already begun to touch the flora, but here in Hiroshima the plants feasted on the heat and on the dead. Only the wind made any noise, weeds and grasses blew against each other. The first reconstruction crews, near what would become the atomic bomb dome, looked like characters in a silent movie. Wood from houses, crumbled granite walls, and the burnt fragments of trees absorbed all other sound. I stood in the middle of the immense, flat, waste of incinerated material. I walked through the whole of the city, first through Kako-machi, then through Kawaguchi-cho, then through Dohashi-cho. I stopped in whatever makeshift hospitals I could find—army canvas tents without electricity or clean water. I explored the ruins of houses, uncovering burnt paintings and clothes, underwear and kimonos, plates, clocks and tables, blown every which way. In a few houses the owners had yet to take their remaining belongings, and they picked through their former domains. "Good afternoon," I bowed to them. "Good afternoon," they bowed back. It seemed inappropriate to say anything more, but they looked at me curiously, as if wondering why I would

59

come to Hiroshima when I so obviously did not belong.

That day, I looked at as much as I could. I walked everywhere (for seeing is the first step to knowing) but what I remember most is not the city, nor the twisted faces, the burnt limbs or the deformed children, or the babies which must have been irradiated in the wombs of their pregnant mothers, or the lipless mouths with teeth crumbling which doctors swabbed with seeming futility. No. That is not what I remember most. For surely you, too, have seen these images on television, in the atomic bomb museums. No. What I remember most about Hiroshima is the woman I saw near the middle of the city. She tried to take a drink of water. She stood along the shore of the river Ota as I walked among the ruins of the Funairi district. She waded into the water until it surrounded her, knee deep. She held a tin cup, drooping in her hand, and dipped her cup into the water. But without possessing the force necessary to stay erect, she fell into the river. She leaned forward and died, then she floated. Her thin corpse meandered down the river. It twirled and rolled. It bumped against the banks. It caught on a pile of bricks, buffeted from side to side, then moved on. And I suspect her body must have floated all the way to the sea, down to the Nasami straits where it was beaten mercilessly by the waves against the rocks.

If I had only radioed Tokyo, if I had never waited, how many people could I have saved?

Now, I am tired. It is late and the house is silent, but I am unable to sleep. I will stay up all night in the kitchen, perhaps making some tea or even drinking some sake. And in the morning I will walk outside onto the tiny balcony behind my house. I will look at the bustling city of Kyoto, moving with its indifferent morning traffic across the bridge to the other side of the river. I will listen for my wife preparing breakfast. But I will not eat with her. I will not be hungry. I will feel completely empty inside. I will look at the green hills in the distance, dark then in shadow. I will squint my eyes. And I will wait desperately for the first rays of the sun to rise.

Murayama Kazuo

Suspended:

Five Stories

Suspended

Thís morning I am sad. I feel sadder than I ever
have the last three and a half months as I walk along the
beach with Alexa. I know that I am not Philip Bonti, and
I know that I think I am Philip Bonti, and if you aren't
who you think you are then you are nothing. "I still don't
have a clue how I got to this island," I tell Alexa. I met
her an hour ago. "They say I must have been vacationing,
or maybe it was work." There is a line—imagine—like the
breakers of the reef just in front of us, and anything before
that line is gone for me, the ocean. And everything after it
is the small life of Philip Bonti.

At breakfast this morning before meeting up with
Alexa I read about the Heaven's Gate cult disaster. The
Kauai newspaper had it on the front page. As far as I'm

concerned they're all freaks and I feel bad for them, but there was one item in all of the news and gossip that got to me. The cultists felt that their bodies were just vessels, like plastic casings which held their trapped inner alien souls in what they saw as the hellfire of earth before those casings would be left as they flew away to the other world. And reading about those casings I know that I am also trapped, only unlike the cultists I'm not caught in the wrong body— my flesh looks the same to me, it has every detail I've felt I've always had—it's my brain that's wrong. I'm trapped in the wrong brain and the key is lost.

"I walk along this beach almost every day where they say they found me," I tell Alexa. I look out at where the reef ripples, at where the rocky oyster-shaped cove opens between the lava cliffs where water smashes, and search for any memory, for any sign of the world before I hit my head. If I could just see that memory, that split-second before I became who I am now, I could pull myself back I think, reattach myself to who I am.

The sand feels heavy beneath me. The glare of the sun tries to wipe out my effort to think back to the past. "They say it was three o'clock with the sun burning its full Hawaiian brightness when they found me." A little boy and girl discovered me. "They didn't look for any immediate clues which might have helped me remember who I am." The young girl was a little older than the boy. She tapped me on my bare shoulder, ran away a few steps, and then came back as her brother picked his nose and gaped at me. "My head hit some rocks in the ocean and my wallet was gone. Maybe I was robbed. I had no identification." Before I saw the boy and girl I remember only water rushing into my nose and beige-white sand.

I am at Alexa's now. We are undressed . . . Each day the beach is different. There are fewer and fewer tourists as we move deeper into the spring. (At least it seems that way to me. My short term memory sluices in and out like white noise on a radio station.) The tourists set up camp with their families and erect sun umbrellas while singles search for lovers.

When I'm at the beach I study the rocks, the Scylla and Charybdis where I might have sunk my windsurfer or dinghy, or maybe I was swimming alone that day. I'm never solo for very long, though. Someone approaches and asks why I'm staring so intently at the ocean. I tell them and it gives me comfort. In the compost of my mind, if I could just tell them exactly how it happened I'd be able to link up to my past.

A number of single women come up to me, some in their late twenties, others a little older in their mid-thirties, almost as alone as I am. They tell me frequently that I am cute. (Philip Bonti seems to be fairly charming even though he must look morose.)

We wend our way back to their hotel or condominium or to their house if they live on the island. Each one feels like some kind of searched-for connection to my past, and Philip Bonti seems to like to have sex more than anything, which means *I* like to have sex.

Alexa tells me she is from Pittsburgh, and for some reason this interests me greatly.

"You know what I really like about Pittsburgh are the neighborhoods," I say.

"You've been there?"

"I think so." I try to remember.

"Oh, right."

"I like the fresh seafood, too," I say emphatically.

She looks at me, baffled. I am full of non sequiturs; little bits of the past push their way through the facade of my singular whole like wafts of air coming up through a sewer grate, only I treasure them because they are who I really am.

"Yeah, I like some of the seafood on the coast of Rhode Island, too," Alexa says covering for me. The air stagnates in her bungalow but it feels a little cooler with her naked beside me. Her skin is smooth and she has strong hips. I want to ask her to describe every kind of seafood she has ever eaten, and then I want her to tell me about every town she has ever seen along the coast of Rhode Island. There are parts of her body that remind me of others, parts which are completely unique, and her short hair, cut in a bob, brings the memory of another face, a pale one that seems so familiar yet ghostlike and unknown.

"How could you have come here without anyone knowing where you are?"

"I don't know." I study an elongated crack in the ceiling. I am truly confused, and I try to run through all the permutations of who what where when and how.

"But someone must have known where you were going. Your mother or brother or sister."

"That's assuming I have a family. I can't assume anything. I have to work from the few possessions I have. There's an FBI agent working on my case and he's been very good. He looks like an agent on TV, tall, impeccably shaved, and always wears a tie. The thing is, you know, everyone thinks we live in the age of Big Brother. But without my wallet I don't have any credit cards or driver's license. I don't know what hotel I was staying at and no one recognized me when the papers ran an article on me. All I know is that I'm not who I think I am, because I think I live at 311 Grandview in the Northwest of D.C. and there is no street like that. And I think that playing the cello has been a lifelong hobby of mine, but I can't play it. And I think I've lived in Italy for a year, but if you ask me what I was doing there, I'll tell you I don't know. And it's one thing after another like that. For a while I even thought I was left-handed, but I'm not."

Alexa runs her hand along my chest and I'm glad she does that. There are too many thoughts coming and I want to jump up and rush outside and walk endlessly until my feet are bleeding. If I could just walk across the island and take in every plant, every wild tropical bird, every waterfall and mile of pavement perhaps something—the tiniest bead of dew on moss or a bird whistling—might ring and shatter prisms of trapped thoughts in my mind.

"Tell me every detail of your neighborhood," I say. "Don't leave anything out."

71

"Where should I start?" she asks, and I am relieved since this is when most women leave me, thinking I'm crazy, when they decide that even on vacation a little escapade with an amnesiac is too much.

Start with your first memory of the neighborhood at age six, I think, but I don't say anything. I lie against the bed board waiting for her to guess what I'm thinking. There must be a central part of me, a core that others can sense by ESP that is the real me.

"When I was eight, I used to steal bubble gum from this small grocery called Dobson's . . ."

I have decided to sail out into the water today. I am all alone. Alexa wanted to come with me, but I told her I needed to make this trip solo. I am going to go out and sail over the breaker into the ocean.

The surf is a little rough this morning, and Alexa told me I should leave it for another day. I can go out and explore tomorrow, she said, but she can't understand that it's not a question of whether I want to go, something inside tells me I must. I've been having sharp headaches lately, a pressure is building inside of me, and I need to relieve it. When I tell the doctor at the public community health center where I am staying, he wants to give me more drugs that will only deaden me senseless. I've tried his hypnosis, his talk therapy and drawings, and nothing has worked.

The boat has a small sail but I move out into the cove easily. The bow bobs up and down on the waves. There are almost no tourists on the wide beach today; the sky is gray, it has rained during the night, and I have the whole coast to myself, the whole world of nature to confront, to beg and to demand back what it has taken from me.

There are old Hawaiian myths of gods ruling the island, and maybe that is how I hit my head, and maybe I need to placate some pagan spirit. But I don't believe life is ruled by any force. It seems more chance, a randomness of cruelty and extreme luck with little reason for one or the other. The only role we play in life is whether we choose to fight against or to accept that chance. (This isn't a small thing either. It can mean the difference between success or failure, between happiness and being a destitute bum on the street.) And maybe that's why I'm sailing out here today. Because if chance is something we can challenge, then I want to claim back my previous self. I want chance to know I won't take anything lying down. I am not going to let myself be some freak in the newspaper or a morass of disparate thoughts.

In front of me the steep, vertically striated lava cliffs, covered with dense plants, pinch towards each other as they attempt to close off the opening to the cove which leads to the wild world of the ocean and to the world of my freedom. I want to scream at those cliffs, and for once, although I have sworn off vengeance, fearing that it will only bring more misery, I let myself. "You fucking pieces of shit," I tell them. "What gives you the right to turn me into an orphan of the world! You're just a stupid piece of inanimate shit."

The rocks, of course, do not respond.

It is getting colder as the wind blows harder and I button up my rubber raincoat. The winds cut back and forth and I have to use my sailing skills to hold the sail and to keep my course straight. I pull the sailboat in just along the cliffs. Scanning the rock, I feel somewhere along this ledge or at that point up above I should be able to find a piece of my clothing, a scrap of my shirt which was torn from my back still clinging to a tiny nub four months later. But there are only rocks and plants so I go in closer. The waves pull in and out this near to the rock, creating a trough which sucks me in. The boat slides sideways, flying down towards the rock, and is barely saved by water swelling up again, lifting the boat high. How close do I need to get, I think, before any secrets will be revealed to me? I let the boat slide and bob nearer and nearer as I scour the face of the rocks. And suddenly the rocks are so close, I am almost touching them. If I don't pull back I will hit them. I tug frantically on the boom, trying to catch some wind along the cliff to give me force to sail out. I lean on the tiller with all my strength. But the water is more powerful. The boat flies high and then comes crashing down. Along the side of the cliff there is a tunnel where water rushes with pulverizing force. The boat strikes the rocks and it is trapped against them. The whole boat leans and I have to jump out or I risk being caught upside down or trapped between the boat and the cliff. I leap into the water and swim as hard as I can, and the current tries to pull me back toward the rocks but I won't let it. Not this time. "I am stronger than you," I shout.

How could you let yourself make such a stupid mistake? I think. You were going to go out over the reef and you let yourself get tempted into the rocks.

But I didn't mean to, I tell myself. You stupid idiot, another voice inside says. It is him, my real self.

I am away from the rock now, bobbing, floating in the warm water of the Pacific. It is raining slightly, but I can see my way back to the shore where the thin line of beige sand rises gently from the oyster-shaped bay, looking safe and secure. I know every inch of that beach from walking along it. But what good is the perspective from there, why look out at the reef when the answer is out here?

I swim toward the reef where the water is breaking. It is a good half mile still and I crawl with my elbows cutting in and out of the water with force.

It is near now, I think. The answer is near. When you get out to the reef you will find out everything. I look at the wide expanse on the other side of the reef. It is enormous and open. The water is unusual today, calmer on the other side of the reef.

When I get to the reef there is a wall of coral before me and I dive down into the water and swim at full speed. I stop in front of the mass of living rock, a barrier of flower like browns and sea anemones. There is no pain under the water, only up above. Down here there is a harmony, a unity to the way that the fish move in choreography. Long fragile corals of pungent orange sway like fans in the gentle current and I hold my breath and dive deeper to a small cave where a grouper is lying, barely more noticeable than a stone along the bottom. If I could only hold my breath forever it wouldn't matter if I was Philip Bonti or not. Only others can say that you aren't who you are. Only the criticisms of newspapers and FBI agents can tell you day after day that something has gone terribly wrong.

I swim into the maze of coral, letting the caverns of arched porous rock leap over and around me like vaults in a Gothic cathedral. A giant sea turtle swims by. A shark comes near and I am worried for a moment, but it seems more afraid of me and kicks away with its triangular tail. Within the crevasses of caves I look for some epiphany. But perhaps the answer is in the fact that no answer comes to me, that no memory comes back to trigger me back to who I was. It may be, I think, as I float suspended, bubbles trickling upward from me in little balloons of air like glass, that the answer is to be who I am now, to accept myself as Philip Bonti. You are Philip Bonti, I think, and I swim under and through corals.

I pop up on the other side of the reef. The air is cold and I feel faint from lack of breath. I'm in the wide open ocean now. But I am not alone. A Coast Guard cutter approaches me and I can see Alexa on the prow of the ship. She is waving, holding a life buoy in her hand.

But you don't understand, it's OK, I'm Philip Bonti, I think. She has a grim look on her face, I can tell when she gets closer. She throws the buoy and the Coast Guard lowers a dinghy to come get me. The FBI agent is with Alexa on deck. They bring me up to them wrapped in a towel and I feel as holy and as at peace as a saint. "I have found out who I really am," I tell Alexa. She whispers for me to be silent. She tells me I'm going to be OK.

"We can put the call through now," a Coast Guard man says to the FBI agent.

"There's a call from your wife," the agent says.

I look at him uncomprehending.

"From Mrs Michelle Corless."

"But I'm Philip Bonti," I say. And they pipe her voice through, crackling, on the open speaker.

Forty

I was trying to get to Africa. The plane had ice all over the wings and the pilot kept reassuring us we would be leaving momentarily, but outside my window thirty-six inches of snow caked the side of the runway, the luggage carriers barely moved, the ground crew stood around like Inuits—a few batted their arms to keep warm—and more snow fell. It was the worst blizzard in twenty-two years: all that snow in twenty-four hours. Power lines downed. The phone line jammed when I'd tried to call the electric company to tell them live wires crossed my street. The only reason I was in the coffin-plane flying to Uganda was because I needed to.

"So where are you headed?" a thin, balding man next to me asked.

"Uganda."

He recoiled.

"What for?"

I pretended to look out the window with such intensity I couldn't hear him. After a while he left me alone and I thought about Jacob, my brother, the one I was going to see. It was Jacob that I needed. Jacob, the one with the biblical name like a prophet, my only sibling. A vision of birthday candles, forty of them on a cake, seemed to float like a faint transparency over the airport runway where gray snow whipped diagonally as the last shadows of sunlight faded and turned into evening. How was I turning forty? The storm outside kept raging (my father had died just a year ago singing opera in the middle of a concert, my mother two years ago sitting on the toilet; we weren't long-lived in my family). At some sudden moment the plane swung out onto the main runway—I could see giant snow blowers whipping piles of snow high into the air, trying to take on nature, to control forces stronger than themselves—it ricketed and whined down the pavement, bumped and barely took off, fighting the inevitable battle, and finally unhinged into the sky.

It was cold up above in the night, so cold even the airplane blankets couldn't keep me warm. Kevin Costner's *Waterworld* sloshed on the movie screen and I started to feel sick, feverish. The balding man next to me snored tremendously and he had terrible breath which was impossible to avoid because he slept with his mouth open. He hadn't taken a shower for weeks either as far as I could tell.

Who knew, I thought, as my throat turned dry and rough the way it always does before one of my bouts of awful sinus headaches (I didn't have a girlfriend anymore or any likely prospects), at forty maybe it was better to be dead.

That's what I thought about for two days all the way to the Entebbe airport, while switching planes in Heathrow where I killed thirteen hours sleeping on a plastic bench. My head ached and I felt totally drugged out as I stepped off the plane into the humid afternoon of the sub-Sahara. I was overdressed with far too many layers of clothes which only made me feel even more that I was trapped, wrapped in a sarcophagus. There's something about stepping off the plane in Africa; it's a complete shock. You leave from one world and enter another. It's not only the weather, I realized later, or that suddenly everyone around you is black, speaking other languages, or even that all of the buildings look old—many of them colonial from around or before World War II while you've just been in a Boeing 747—it's that the whole mentality and time and even the smell of the tree bark is different and you're the odd one out. I was almost ready to turn right around and head back to the East Coast, but that was when I saw my brother waving to me.

"Of course I feel like a failure," I told my brother. I had been in the country a day and a half. It takes a while to get around to what's really on your mind, even with a close sibling. We were all alone except for the sound of tropical birds, drinking beer in a remote campsite on an island in a lake in western Uganda where my brother was working for the Jane Goodall Society reintroducing chimps to the wild. "I don't do anything that requires an ounce of intelligence," I said. "I just put the stuff in: install the software, connect the cables. I'm like a modern plumber ... The only good thing about plumbers is that they know how to do the obvious. Like last week, for example, this woman called me in to her office because she said the fax unit on her computer wasn't working. I went over and checked the computer out and everything seemed to be fine, so I said, 'Why don't you show me how you usually fax.' She said, 'Well, like I told you I've never been able to fax because the machine isn't working.' I said, 'Well just show me.' So she pulled out a piece of paper and put it against the computer screen and started rubbing it up and down across the monitor. And then she gave me this puzzled look and said, 'See? It won't work.'"

Jacob smiled.

"And a few weeks before that I met some woman who told me she thought the computer mouse was great but it was really hard to use. 'Why don't they make it easier?' she asked, 'My foot gets tired.' I swear to god this is all true."

Jacob leaned back in his director's chair.

"So you came all the way out to Uganda because of that?"

"How can you say that?" I glanced away from him out over the lake. "Of course I didn't come just because of that. I came because of everything."

"Like what?"

"Like everything," I shouted. "Don't you see?"

He turned quiet and pensive, the way he always does just before he has something big to say that's on his mind.

"Well what's the big deal?" he finally demanded. "So you're forty and you have a shitty job, but you can change all of that."

"But I can't. That's just the thing. I can never go back to being under forty, and everything in my life feels paralyzed. Completely frozen. I might as well have polio."

"What are you talking about?"

"I'm talking about everything! I'm talking about Katie leaving me after four years, about dad dying last year, mom gone and you all the fucking way out here. Turning forty and celebrating my birthday last week with no one I even care about."

"So what happened with Katie? Why did you break up with her?"

The beer tasted bitter.

"I told you, I didn't break up with her she broke up with me. I told you everything in the letter I sent."

"What letter?"

Jacob picked off a piece of one of his rough nails.

"You mean you didn't get it? Well what kind of fucking postal service do they have in this country?"

"Maybe it got lost in the States."

"Yeah, and the Pope's Gwyneth Paltrow."

"So what happened?"

"She just left. Said she knew she'd never want to marry me—that it was better to stop living together and get it over with sooner rather than later."

"She's probably right."

I jumped up and walked around the dusty camp.

"Is that all you have to say?"

"You're going to be better off without her."

"How would you know? You don't even really understand how I feel about her."

"I just know you always said there were problems that couldn't be resolved."

"That's what you always think, that you know everything," I said and I downed an entire beer. I was all alone, I knew then. Truly all alone. Who said no man can be an island unto himself? Every man is like an island.

86

Later that night I had an incredible urge. I woke up in my hut as moonlight flashed through the rafters; the light was astonishingly bright. I saw a pair of eyes glowing above me and then the eyes darted and a black object jumped stealthily away. I put on a pair of shorts and a T-shirt and stepped out past my brother. Most of Africa is farms and a few big cities these days, but this island is in the middle of nowhere, a special game reserve not even marked on maps.

Something moved in one of the trees and I followed the sound of the tree sway, stumbling a little on some thick roots. The air was cool this time of night and I shivered, the ground was moist. It was hard to tell exactly where the animal was jumping, but I did my best to keep up with its giant leaps. Staring up at the top of the trees, running and cutting back and forth in wild zigzags, it wasn't long before I was far away from camp deep into the island. I thought I was following a chimp, but I wasn't sure. Branches looked silver and ebony in the night as they whipped and snapped past me and into my face. I cut my wrist on some sharp vines and scarred my cheek. Just when I thought the animal was going to stop, that I had actually run it down—because it paused and I couldn't hear any tree branches moving—the animal let out a ferocious screech, showed flashes of pointy teeth. The animal shook the high tree branches jumping up and down mocking me, telling me that I didn't belong here either. It screeched louder and then in a higher voice. Other similar primal screams joined in from different animals. I turned around trying to locate the other animals, and suddenly the whole forest went silent. The absence of cacophony. You could have heard termites walking. There was nothing but moonlight and high trees and mainly darkness.

What's going on here? I thought. A couple of zebras ran through the forest, cracking branches. I crouched behind a big tree and peeked out behind the trunk. An elephant and then another and then yet another crashed and trumpeted nearby, oblivious to me in the woods. The size of their immense bodies, the hugeness of so much muscle and their curved ivory tusks pushed me down even lower behind the tree. Packs of animals ran through the forest, things I would never have been able to recognize even in broad daylight: pig-like boars with stiff bouncing tails, birds swarming in flight, deer-like animals with strange upward thrusting horns, fox-like jackals, wild dogs.

I froze even though I knew I should run.

A male lion with a thick mane and then a lioness and then a group of six lions with cubs strutted forward into a clearing. The head of the pride held fresh meat in his mouth, the lions fifty or sixty feet away. I could still have moved to safety. I dropped to my knees and hid beneath a bush where I thought I would lie until the morning came; for days if necessary, or weeks, or until I could slip away if the lions turned their attention elsewhere. But I didn't stay under that bush. An impulse to get up took over me, and since impulses come from within I can only try to explain my movement this way: from somewhere deep inside, from the back of my brain or even deeper in the primitiveness of the nervous system in the hypothalamus or even pre-thought in my heart, my body said, confront death, the fact that you are no longer a kid, the boredom of your office existence, your directionlessness, your paralysis, your sense of shame at losing Katie, wondering why she no longer feels attracted to you; reinvigorate yourself with life.

I lumbered up and walked toward the lions, wanting to see how close I could get. If I had been conscious, fully in control of myself, it would have been crazy I know. It would have been suicidal. But it didn't feel that way to me. What it felt like was an irresistible attraction, being pulled close to something like pilgrims needing to touch a holy relic to be saved. The mere sight of the lions filled me with a sense of longing to touch one. The lions didn't notice me at first. How could they have? They had their meat and as the kings and undisputed masters of the jungle why would they expect a lesser creature to stick around when even elephants ran before them? I drank in the power of each perfectly honed animal. Each radiated strength, a sense of purpose, the pride of supremacy, and also shared with the others, was loved by the others. The lionesses picked up cubs by the scruff of their necks when they strayed too far. The males licked wounds from the hunt off each other. The pride was a single living organism, each part bringing food and oxygen to the other. Not one could be left behind or would be left behind. Not one would sit alone in a bar drinking Guinness waiting for the end of a horrible day, for the bartender to close up. Not one would have to wonder after forty years what it was all fucking for. Forty years gone. One half ticked away. Fear of heading towards the end but no sense of what the value of the first half was in any case. Eat another meal. Sleep another day. The weekend. Wait for the weekend. Always waiting for the weekend and for some tiddlywinks of entertainment to make me smile for just five minutes.

I wanted to touch one. I came near to one of the male lions, and when I was close enough he saw me. His eyes flashed yellow-green in the night. He came up to me, took one swipe with his immense paw. I stepped back. He roared. Every one of his muscles mounded, completely articulated. His tail cut the air. He prepared to leap. And suddenly I knew this wasn't a game, some *National Geographic* nature fantasy. Don't cry, I told myself, just don't cry he'll smell the fear. But I couldn't help myself. I started to bawl uncontrollably. My face felt hot and I stepped slowly backwards. The lion let me go for a ways. Then I stumbled briefly, just so briefly, on the edge of a bush behind me. The lion rushed forward at full speed as if my stumble had been the cue to start race horses out of a gate. He took three bounds and hit me full in the chest. The force pressed my ribs. Air flew out of me. I felt knocked by a train. I hit the ground. My body felt heavy and I couldn't think, I felt only pain. The lion circled around me. It paced and rounded. It moved its large Herculean body as I prayed to God even though I don't believe in God. And then, from somewhere in the distance, lights flashed and shots were fired, a group of men came closer and the lions ran off. My brother called for a first-aid kit as he ran up to me and touched me gently. "Jesus," he said, "he's bleeding." The men yelled out instructions to each other in Swahili. One dark man looked over me and said he was a doctor, and they carried me away as I gazed up half-conscious at the trees.

*   *   *

When I was in college I used to read Greek tragedies. I liked them because there was always catharsis, revelation, clarity. I liked the sound of the words. I would read the plays out loud, even in Greek, although I didn't understand a syllable of the language. But my professors seemed more interested in obscure analysis. Every time they spoke of the plays the words seemed to die in front of me. It was the same in most of my other classes, and eventually I dropped out. For a while I thought I could be an opera singer like my father, but then I realized I didn't have the talent. After I was done wandering—living here and there working odd jobs—I got my gig installing computers.

Nothing in life, though, seems as clear as in those Greek plays. (At the end of the *Eumenides*, Athena sets everything straight.)

My plane landed in Boston and the snow had melted, but a new gale, a nor'wester was sweeping up the coast, and I locked myself into my tiny apartment. I watched the Weather Channel and placed a bucket in my bathroom where the roof leaked, which my landlord refused to fix. On top of my video player, which I had bought third-hand, I found an old black and white movie *High Sierra* that I had forgotten to finish and return before leaving. It must have been three weeks overdue.

Jacob had been furious with me. He said I could have killed myself. I think he felt I was a complete burden the whole time, although he did his best to help me.

I lay on my bed uncomfortably, listening to the rain, and picked up the phone and called Katie. A man answered and I felt paranoid that she was already involved with someone else and hung up. The movie continued when I turned it on, just near the climax. Humphrey Bogart, an outlaw, was trapped against a high granite cliff while cops came in around him. A sharp shooter high above was trying to kill him, but before Bogart dies he's cocky, confident, proud.

I saw the lion again, so close, me next to it in the forest. And for a moment I felt more powerful than an

atomic bomb, more serene than a lake. I shut off the lights
and video and listened to the rain. It was completely dark
in the room. The sound was rhythmic, soothing, and I
hoped it would rain for days.

Shanghaied

J ared finally had two weeks of vacation. He had been working solidly for the last twelve months and now he was on his way to China. No more voice mail, no more projects to be completed, no more trying to figure out which clothes to wear in the morning. Before he left his apartment he checked to see he had enough money, and the looseness of his jeans and T-shirt under a sweater felt awkward for a Monday morning and wonderful.

At the United terminal he met his co-worker Adriana. "You look great," he told her.

"You look like a mess."

The terminal was busy, bodies rushing here and there to get to their gates on time, but a pocket of calm surrounded the two of them. On the plane, where they were upgraded to business class because they had bought their tickets together on a two-fer promotional, Jared was sipping some champagne, leaning back in the wide comfortable seat, when he noticed Adriana had a new ring. "When did you get that?" he asked.

"Do you like it?"

"Let me see. It's nice."

It was twenty-two-carat gold with a small delicate diamond.

"Zack gave it to me last week."

He thought he should have noticed it earlier since they worked so near each other at GE. He was one of the new young engineers on the Zephyr 629 helicopter, and she was responsible for co-handling the public relations side of the project.

"It's too bad he couldn't come," Jared said.

"Yeah, too bad Martha couldn't come too. But you've gotta take the vacations when they give 'em to you."

"I know, but this taking of time when the other one can't . . ."

"It's true, but better something than nothing."

"So what are you going to do after Shanghai?" Jared asked. He finished his glass and poured some more. The stewardess had left the rest of the bottle for the two of them.

"I'm going to this city called Suzhou. It's supposed to be the Venice of China. Canals, old gardens."

"Sounds great but won't the gardens be kind of dead in the middle of January?"

Adriana looked at the Fodor's on her open tray table and traced circles of water. Her smile, which had been so permanent before—he had noticed her smile especially since she wore bright red lipstick and since Martha never wore lipstick—was gone. "Well, who knows. What about you?"

"I don't know. It depends on what I find. Hard to say."

He poured her another and she poured him one. The plane purred, there was very little turbulence and the captain announced *Air Force One* would be the first movie selection.

"I guess they have two movies because the flight's so long," Adriana said. She grinned a champagne grin. "Here's to our vacation." She toasted, spilling a little on her skirt of fine gray wool. Her turtleneck went well with her hair and eyes he thought.

"Yeah, to our few days of freedom."

Either she didn't notice the champagne she'd spilled or she ignored it. When the stewardess came around later she bought some Cartier perfume from the duty-free shop and he bought a bottle of Glennfidich.

"Isn't that going to be heavy?" she asked. "Why not buy it on the way back?"

"Because I want to drink it in China."

She was starting to bother him with her cautious motherliness. It was good they'd have only one day together in Shanghai. After that they wouldn't meet up until the flight home.

At the airport in Shanghai they waited by the carousel until the last bags went round and round and Adriana's bag didn't arrive. They filled out the paperwork, but the Chinese man working for United barely spoke English. He grunted when Adriana asked him when the next flight with her bag might come in and whether they would deliver it to her hotel.

"Is there a manager I can speak to?"

"I am manager."

They went through customs and immigration where soldiers scrutinized their passports as if they were criminals trying to break into the country.

"Jesus," Adriana said on their way to a taxi, "it's not as if I'd want to stay here permanently. I mean Christ, I don't even have any clothes."

"The bag will probably come tomorrow."

"Yeah, but what if it doesn't?"

"It's all right. Everything's all right. Just remember, we're on vacation."

"I guess this will give me an excuse to go shopping. I want to get some silk things."

When they arrived at the taxi stand there were so many people rushing up, and not enough vehicles, that people cut in line. A man in full police uniform whistled for taxis to come forward but no one seemed to pay any attention. Jared and Adriana stepped into a taxi and an older woman and her son shoved in on the other side. "This our taxi," the older woman said.

"No, we were here first," Jared said.

"No, we here." The son was dressed in a prep-school blue blazer, his hair neatly combed back.

"How about if we share?" Jared asked.

The woman barked at the driver. The driver yelled out to another passing cab and the woman told Adriana and Jared to get into the other taxi. She wasn't going to budge and the driver of the first taxi took off with her and her son.

On their way through the streets of Shanghai Jared couldn't believe he was finally in China. Ever since he was a kid he'd wanted to come. Bicycles crowded around the taxi as they navigated a large boulevard where a banner stretched across the road proclaiming, "Welcome to Shanghai! 1997 Year of the Tourist."

Adriana checked in at the long marble counter of the Peace hotel, a 1920s art deco classic, a remnant of colonial days. The man behind the counter told her their room was three twenty-eight.

"And my room?" Jared asked.

"I'm sorry?" The man spoke in a trained British accent.

"We're supposed to have two rooms."

"You are not Mr and Mrs Moss?"

"No, that's Adriana Moss. There should be another room for me."

The receptionist informed him all of the rooms were full and that there was no indication two rooms had been requested. Adriana demanded to speak to someone in charge, but Jared told her it was OK, he would find another room at a different hotel.

"No, you're tired. They should get you a room here."

The man behind the counter shook his head. Jared *was* tired and it was dark and raining outside.

"Why don't you just stay with me?" Adriana asked.

He thought about his alternatives. "Are you sure?"

"Of course, I'm sure. It's no big deal."

There was a fully stocked bar in the room, long curtains made of red velvet, the bedspreads had a British floral pattern, and two brass and wood fans dangled from the high decorated ceiling. "I can't believe it," Adriana said. "It's like it's out of some Humphrey Bogart movie."

Jared uncorked a crystal bottle of bourbon. The room was luxurious but it was inexpensive by American standards. He filled a nice highball and made one for Adriana. Her hair was wet, all messed up, and she looked good as he gave her the drink.

"Let's get trashed," she said. "You know, I haven't gotten really drunk for years."

He thought she didn't seem like the type to get plastered.

"I mean hell, we're on vacation aren't we?"

He drank his bourbon. The bourbon was good.

"Don't you feel like you're getting old?" she said. "I mean, suddenly you get to be a couple of years over thirty and it looks like everything's going the other way."

"I don't know. Everything seems to be going more or less my way."

"Well maybe it's different for you, but I certainly

don't feel that way." She leaned across one of the queen-size beds.

"I'm not saying it's perfect," Jared said. "Just that things seem more or less OK."

"And that's enough for you?"

It was funny, he hadn't thought about Martha since leaving the States. He held his glass up to the light and looked at the amber whiskey. Adriana was starting to seem a little sad to him. He knew it was rude to appear so distracted when someone else was in the room, but he was. "I think I'm going to try to go to the Chinese opera tonight," he said.

"Can I come along?"

He paused and then said, "Sure."

"It's OK. I'll stay here. I think I just want to stay here."

"No, come along. Come on, let's go."

"Are you positive?"

"Positive."

"You're sure?"

"Sure."

There were neon lights along the main street for more than a mile in bubble gum pinks, key lime greens and pomegranate reds. "That was incredible," Jared said after the opera.

"Yeah."

"Let's go to a bar. I think I could use a drink now. I finally feel like I'm on vacation. You know what I mean?

I mean we could never have seen anything like that in Boston. Ever."

"I know." Adriana walked close beside him.

Bicyclists roamed everywhere even at this time of night. A tough-looking man with a black leather jacket hawked a couple of prostitutes. People milled about looking at gold jewelry and electronic goods. "It's definitely not what I thought a Communist country would be like," Jared said. Old men spoke loudly, eating peanuts, spitting at street corners while young people shouted out of bars, drunk.

"It's kind of like the Wild West," Adriana said.

Why did people have to make comparisons? Jared wondered. Why couldn't something just be what it was? Adriana was so dependable, safe, just like everyone else in the office.

"How about if we go to that bar over there?" Adriana said.

A man dressed nineteen-thirties style, a gangster type with a pin-striped suit and a wide Panama guarded the door, only letting in people who had money. Live disco surged around them when they entered. Three women with pink sequined dresses backed up two male singers on a revolving stage. The floor was lit up with multi-colored lights under clear fiberglass. Mirror balls flashed around the room over the collection of bodies; there was barely enough space to move, but they forced themselves into the crowd after Jared bought some drinks.

Adriana drank hers and he drank his, he got two more, they danced, and then he got a couple more, a couple more and a couple more. A young Chinese woman came up to him and pulled at the lapel of his shirt. She whispered something into his ear he couldn't quite hear. Her hair was long and she had a smooth face, not round, unusual for someone Chinese he thought; her eyes were lightly highlighted. She pulled him aside and said, "You come with me. Leave that woman."

"She's not my wife. She's not even my girlfriend."

"So why you not come with me?"

"I have to tell her I'm leaving." He hadn't felt this drunk in ages as he went up to Adriana. She was dancing with another man. She seemed to be doing fine for herself.

"I'm gonna go," he said.

"Where?"

"I don't know."

"With who?" but he knew she already knew so he said nothing.

"Are you sure you can make it home all right?" she ribbed him.

"I was just going to ask the same of you." He became serious.

"Yeah, I'll take care of myself loverboy. And I promise I won't tell anyone back home either."

Later that night at three in the morning as he walked back to the Peace hotel he thought about what a strange place the woman had taken him to. They had stumbled for what seemed like hours through old Shanghai. Narrow passageways barely wide enough for two traced arteries through a labyrinth of buildings. He would have become lost instantly if it hadn't been for her arm around him. Wooden stalls of a permanent outdoor market lined the streets. A bare light bulb lit up a store where watches and machines were repaired, sewing machines receding into a dark back room where a lone man worked. Dry goods stores displayed bags of rice. Cured duck and pork hung forlornly in the windows. He walked in a bazaar shut for the evening, the stalls and windows locked, the place deserted, left in its silent dirty aftermath with only a touch of moonlight and an occasional drunk passerby to keep the place from complete extinguished death. The ground smelled like manure. Here and there, when they came to a more open area where two streets met, a cart lay abandoned and at one intersection a donkey was tied up to a cart. He saw a thick metal cauldron next to the donkey and it smelled like boiled fat. Wet straw with mud littered the ground. They turned a corner of a narrow street and came to a wide open square with a pond in the middle, and in the middle of the pond a wooden classical building, octagonal with a pagoda roof, floated up out of the water.

"It's beautiful," he said. He thought this is what she had dragged him all the way there for, but he knew this wasn't the case since she kept putting her hand into his front pocket. She was feeling him up and he was drunk, and he didn't really care what happened. He wanted to take it all in, everything, the dirtiness of old Shanghai like the opulence of the Peace hotel.

"My home is near here," she said, and they went back

into the narrow streets, only they were different now; they began to straighten out, the old buildings replaced by tall twenty-story concrete boxes one after another in endless rows. In the moonlight he saw clothes-lines full of laundry, fluttering rags whipping overhead. It was cold and dank. The concrete of the buildings was falling apart. They went into one of the boxes and walked up a dark staircase sixteen stories. She opened one of the doors, and they came into a small room with coal soot on the walls and an old man, withered, lay wheezing on a cot.

"Come back here," she said. She opened a purple worn cloth door leading to the back of the room. He looked at the old man coughing, unable to sleep. The old man looked at him, his eyes glassy, and he didn't seem to see him, he appeared to look through him.

"It's OK," she laughed leading him into the back. "It's my grandfather. He can't hear." She stopped laughing abruptly. She started to unbutton his shirt. She rubbed her hands along his chest and pulled him down onto the bed and started to lick him below but he got up. He was disgusted with himself. He thought of Martha, he thought of the old man. He left a large amount of money.

"I don't know what the fuck we're doing here," Adriana said when he came back to the hotel room; she was huddled in a ball crying.

"I know."

"They took everything I have. My purse, everything."

"Who?"

"What kind of vacation is this? I just want to go back to America where everything is safe."

"What happened?"

"Some guy, he took everything. I don't know. Fuck, I feel sick."

He went to her bed and put his hand on her forehead. She was hot and sweaty and he rubbed her gently like a cat. She quieted down and he looked out the tall windows of the bedroom, out over the moonlit endless dark blue wasteland of Shanghai. She must have opened the curtains and stood by the window before, he thought. His head hurt, too. He felt very dehydrated. He turned off the light on the bed stand and the room turned into shadows, suffused with the blueness of the outside, the color of black mixed with indigo. He pulled the covers back and placed Adriana gently into bed, then he took off his shoes and socks and went into bed beside her. He placed his arm around her and lay with his pants and shirt on next to her, feeling her slowly sob then calm down.

"What am I going to tell Zack?" she said.

"I don't know. Tell him next time he should come on vacation with you."

He could already feel himself back in the office at work. They would travel together tomorrow, he thought. He didn't know what he would tell Martha. He tried to close his eyes to sleep but every time he looked up at the ceiling it seemed to spin. He was on vacation he kept telling himself. Everything in his life was OK. Where was Martha? Why wasn't she with him? He went to sleep finally and dreamed he was all alone on a deserted island. A coconut fell on him. He grew old, the coconut tree died, he went into a long sleep and then woke up one day after a thousand years but no one ever came to rescue him.

In the middle of the night he woke up suddenly. He kissed Adriana, and she kissed him back.

Banana Bat

N oel and Katrina went down to Costa Rica for
their honeymoon. They had already been living together
for four years and neither one really liked the word honeymoon. For Noel it made him think of ancient fertility
rituals, and he didn't want kids. For Katrina, she had told
him, it just made her think of a big pot of honey. But Noel
definitely wanted something to mark their time of marriage.

In Costa Rica, Noel's grandfather picked them up.
Before the trip, back in New York, Katrina had fought with
Noel about why they had to go stay with his grandfather.
"Because he's getting old," Noel had said. "I've probably
seen him only three or four times in my life. I want to get
to know him better. It'll be somewhere new and amazing,
and he's offered to have us."

"How about because it's free?" Katrina said. "You're so goddamn tight. Your grandfather bribes you with a free trip and you practically cum in your pants."

"OK. Because it's cheaper, too. But money doesn't exactly grow on trees."

"I know," Katrina mimicked, "and you're a fledgling architect and I'm a grad student. It's the same old line Noel. It gets tiring." Later that night she went out and bought a Hermès scarf just to tweak him.

At the airport Noel's grandfather, Jack, met them and took them into the hills. When they arrived at their final destination his house worker took their bags inside, but before they could go into the house Jack insisted on giving them a tour of the grounds.

"Not a bad life, the life of an ex-pat," Katrina said as they walked through the garden. Noel cringed. Her voice was laced with sarcasm. She'd been giving his grandfather crap the whole way from the airport, telling him how nice it must be to have cheap labor around to exploit.

"Yes, it's pretty comfortable down here." He seemed to ignore her innuendo, and Noel liked his grandfather's poise. He towered, a tall sturdy man, with healthy cheeks, brown eyes, hair combed back, and worn faded jeans. He looked like a Rock Hudson type.

"I've got a thousand birds out here," he said. Bird cages sprouted everywhere. Some hung from big tropical trees, others rested on bird-bath stands. The whole back yard, big and carefully mowed, fluttered with bird calls.

"How did you get them all?" Noel asked.

Katrina poked a finger through one of the bigger cages where a four-foot cockatoo grappled bamboo with its beak. The bird appeared curious to Noel. It seemed intelligent, focusing its eyes clearly on his, and flashed a coy smile.

"You have to be careful about putting your hands in there," Jack said. "That one is named Molly. She's pretty sexy."

"I didn't know birds could be sexy," Katrina said.

"Well, Molly can."

"I bet they like it in their cages," she said.

"Actually, I've heard that birds can live twice or three times as long in a cage as in the wild," Noel said.

"No, I bet she's right. It probably isn't very comfortable. But ultimately, I want to look at them, so they're here."

Katrina hurried ahead to a much smaller cage with a brown ugly bird inside. Noel felt good close to his grandfather. He was the kind of man you could gain inspiration from. The pink stucco house held a low profile with a red tiled roof. It was wide and two storied, tressed with hanging red flowered plants, complete with a big covered patio. He could already taste a cool gin and tonic while sitting on the porch watching the sun set.

Katrina probed her finger inside the cage and the bird latched on to her. She shouted and the bird held tight as they ran up to her. It was a banana bat, Jack said, and Noel watched in horror, uncomfortable with the sight of blood, fearful for Katrina as his grandfather ripped open the cage, grabbed the bird by its wings, and lifted it off.

"They'll do that sometimes," he said. "But I've had the bat tested for rabies. It's harmless."

"You're such a hypochondriac," Noel said. "Just because you come from some smart-ass intellectual family and you think my grandfather's some fat cat industrialist from Chicago living off the fat of the land doesn't mean you can ruin our whole trip because of some bat bite."

Katrina muttered something.

"What's that?"

"Nothing."

"No, what did you say?"

"I said, sometimes I wonder why I married you."

"Oh Jesus, Katrina. You're so spoiled." He remembered a photo of her at the age of twelve, riding on her father's shoulders; she was already far too old for anything like that, but her father would give her everything.

"And you're so overbearing. We never even would have come here if you hadn't insisted. We could have been in Hawaii somewhere. Or in Bozeman with Mikey and Del."

"Yeah, but we did come here and you agreed to come. Look, let's just go down to dinner and forget everything."

"No, I'm not going to forget about everything because I'm hurt."

Her father had died a year ago from AIDS, a hemophiliac, leaving her without any parents, and he knew it was hard on her. She could barely sleep sometimes. She would wake up in the middle of the night, crying.

"Well, where does it hurt?"

"Right *here*."

"Let me see."

She removed her Band-Aid and the tip of her index finger looked slightly swollen.

"See, it looks awful. So don't just tell me it's all in my mind because it's not."

"OK, it's not all in your mind. But it doesn't look that bad. We'll see a doctor tomorrow."

She started to cry. It was ten o'clock at night and the room was ill-lit by a lone bulb hanging from the center of the ceiling.

"I could be dying of something by then. I need to get back to New York. I've got to get back to a hospital now."

"Are you kidding?"

"No, I'm not kidding."

"But it's nothing."

"You wouldn't be saying that if it was you who was bitten."

"You're completely hysterical. I can't take it anymore. You're totally irrational."

"Well then find me a doctor *now*."

"Right here? Fifteen miles from the nearest town?"

"Yeah, right here. Right now."

Before marrying, Noel and Katrina had already broken up once. A year and a half ago they'd gotten back together. That night, sleeping together for the first time in seven months, they'd made wonderful love. They had engaged in numerous positions, and in the end Noel pushed from behind and Katrina moaned and Noel exhausted himself. Afterwards, as they lay on the bed, first in complete ecstatic silence and then talking Noel said, "I think opposites *do* attract." He felt her soft breasts. "I mean, look at us."

"I don't know," Katrina said.

"What do you mean?"

"If we were really opposites we never would have gotten together in the first place." She propped herself on a pillow against the wall.

"You're thinking too much." He rubbed her stomach. "Let's stop thinking."

"You're the one who brought it up in the first place." She kissed him.

"All I know is that I don't want to have any more fights. I don't want to be apart from you anymore."

"So let's not have any more fights." She placed the onus on him. He didn't want to talk anymore. He ran his fingers through her hair and she scratched his back. She was so smart he thought. Tough and beautiful. She looked like a dancer. She could be a ballet dancer if she wanted to. She could be a construction worker with an immense bulldozer or a mathematician for NASA.

"In my opinion," the doctor said with a Costa Rican accent, examining her finger more closely, inspecting it again and pondering, "I don't think it's a problem." Katrina pulled her finger out of his hand. "But again, it's just in my opinion. Maybe you want another opinion?"

The doctor was a roly-poly man with a thick brown mustache. He lived five miles from Jack's house, down a long dirt road where Noel had gone to fetch him.

"You are very lucky though, Señora. This man here, Don Jack, he is a great man. Everyone in the community likes him. You can rest and relax here. Your hand will get better. You won't have any problems. This casa is called Saludad, meaning health."

"Thanks for coming so late," Noel said, "I'll take you right home."

In front of the doctor's house Noel paid him and rushed back to Katrina. The house was completely silent when he returned. He felt calmer now and he thought: so this is what marriage is like. Running out to get a doctor at night. It was different from just living with someone. He liked the feeling of responsibility for another person. They'd been married in a civil ceremony, and there had been no one except a justice of the peace, but they had said their vows. In the middle of the vows the words "in sickness and in health" had stuck with him. It had been as if he were watching his own wedding, seeing himself commit to such an awesome responsibility through an ancient rite of union which didn't seem to work for almost anyone anymore, and he had felt fear and elation.

He looked at his grandfather's art, old oil paintings of Spanish conquistadors, modern watercolors of New York, and even one by Georgia O'Keefe of a wild red poppy.

"That was your grandmother's choice," his grandfather had told him earlier. "I never did like O'Keefe. Too flowery. But Jean insisted on having it."

Noel went upstairs to their bedroom. He could hear Katrina breathing softly and rhythmically and he was glad she was sleeping. He took off his clothes as quietly as possible, entered the bed surprised at how thick the blankets were, and realized that it could, in fact, get cool in the evening this far south. She rested calmly beside him, the house completely silent; she turned towards him seemingly in her sleep, and in a groggy voice she said suddenly, "I don't trust him. I still want to go home."

The next morning it was raining incredibly hard. "So what do you want to do?" Noel asked. "Let's start celebrating our honeymoon."

"How could you be so insensitive?" Katrina said. Noel got dressed while she lay propped up in bed. "I mean, I think it's great that they have a local doctor nearby, and I bet he's good at what he does given his training, but I need to see a specialist. We've got to go into San José."

Noel zipped up his jeans. His grandfather had a beautiful armoire carved out of solid hazel wood from the seventeenth century and he wanted to ask him the story of how he'd acquired it. He wanted to know more about the local Indians too. How they were treated, whether they had mixed completely or whether there were still separate areas like reservations in the US. He wanted to ask him how the rain forests were holding up. "And then what?" Noel said.

"What do you mean?"

"And then what would you want to do after that?"

Katrina's hair fell long and uncombed around her white nightgown.

"You're not taking this whole thing seriously. You're smirking."

It was weird, Noel thought, they hadn't made love for three days now.

"Yes I am smirking, because you look great when you're mad."

"Fuck you, Noel. Just fuck you."

"Well what do you want me to say? My grandfather says the bat is harmless. The doctor says your finger is fine. The road is probably washed out half way to San José. And even if we went, you'd say you want to go back to New York because you wouldn't trust the doctor in San José either, and because what you're really mad about isn't even your finger, it's that we're with my grandfather and because getting bitten reminds you that your father died of a sudden illness, and because—"

"You think you know everything don't you? That you're the only one who can understand anything."

"No, it's not that I think I know everything. It's just that I think you should relax a little, that we should enjoy our honeymoon, and that everything's going to be OK."

He hurried up to her and put his arm around her. She pushed him away and kicked at her blankets and threw on the first clothes she could find, went downstairs and demanded the keys to the Jeep from Jack. The rain fell like quarters as she went outside. The water splashed in large splotches on her blue cotton sweater and Noel ran after her as she raced the engine, sending sickly pale smoke up into the air. The door on the passenger side wouldn't yield as she started to pull away and he thought she was going to leave him, but she paused for a moment, as if wondering whether she should let him in, then opened the door, and he climbed inside. He said nothing to her for a long while as they raced down the long road to San José, spraying water into the forest.

"Watch out!" Noel said. They had just come over the rise of a tiny hill, the pavement on this part of the road spiked up and down, it was impossible to see more than a hundred feet ahead, and at the bottom of the current dip a pool of water, like a river, flowed across the road. Katrina slammed on the brakes. The Jeep slid sideways but mostly forward. The whole unstoppable velocity gave a tremendous feeling of weight to the vehicle, a millisecond sensation of ineluctable predestination, and Noel braced his arms against the dashboard as they hit the water. The water stopped the Jeep cold. It deflected the Jeep like a wall and sent them diagonally off the road and into the forest. When the Jeep came to rest it stood miraculously upright Noel thought, though the top plastic and canvas covering had somehow come off. The engine was extinguished by the water. The only sound was the sound of the forest, a quietness of high canopied trees with splatters of rain falling from the great tops.

Noel unbraced himself and checked to see if Katrina

was all right. She lay with her head and arms draped over the steering wheel. "Don't start," she said.

"Don't start what?"

"Don't start telling me I should have done something different than I did because I couldn't."

"I wasn't going to say anything. I was just going to ask if you're all right." A big drop of rain splattered on his forehead.

"Of course I'm not all right. My finger hurts." She raised her bandaged finger like a deathly battle wound. Her hand was red, perhaps from the fright, and looked naked in the rain.

"I know, but how about the rest of you?"

"What difference does it make? Why is the rest of me more important than my finger?"

Noel wanted to get out and walk around. He wanted to walk deep into the forest alone, far from the Jeep.

"It's not." He stepped outside.

"But that's not what *you* think. Because in one case *you* think it makes sense for me to be hurt, and in the other *you* think it doesn't. It all has to depend on what *you* think . . . All I'm saying Noel is that you should trust me. If I think something's some way different than what you think then maybe I have a reason."

It was slightly cold but he felt he could walk for miles into the forest letting himself get wet and that he would feel purified by such a walk.

"What does any of this have to do with the accident we just had? With whether you're all right? Or with why you've been so grumpy the whole time we've been down here."

"What I'm saying Noel, is that I'm not going to cave in all the time. What I'm saying is that I'm going to be *with* you, but I'm not going to be under you. You think you asked me if I wanted to come down here, but you never really even asked me. You think you don't want to have kids, and you think we've talked about this and resolved this, but even when you've talked to me you've never really let anything sink in. And you think yesterday when you went and got the doctor that you were going and doing a big favor for me, but what you should have realized was that you were really doing it for *us*. There *is* no just you or me now. We have to be separate but one."

Noel looked at Katrina and she was crying. She was crying from the honesty and intensity of what she was saying, he thought. He had never seen her this way, so vulnerable and yet so strong at the same time. He wanted just to walk away. He wanted to go up to her and comfort her, and the tug between the two emotions kept him motionless, his feet planted firmly in a collection of rotting wet leaves and mud. He thought that she was too sensitive. He thought that he didn't understand how her finger could be hurting her so much or how she could be so rude to his grandfather and then expect him not to be rude to her, or how any of that could have any relevance after crashing a Jeep and then surviving.

He walked around the Jeep and went up to her side. He opened the door and crouched down so that he could look at her crying face, which she turned away from him.

"Let's walk," he said, and he put his arm around her, "if you want to. Let's walk to San José and I'll try to work on it."

It was raining harder now. The rain came down in a wall and the stream of water which they had hit with the Jeep flowed wide. "I don't know if we can cross it," Katrina said, and she grabbed hold of his hand. She kissed him. He didn't care about anything now, the Jeep or his grandfather. He didn't want to think about anything. He looked up at the sky, gray and white, a wash above the trees. The rain crashed down hard on his face. It felt good and cold. He closed his eyes against the rain. He let the sweet and salty taste of the water splatter into his mouth. He held Katrina's hand in the rain and felt the heavens pour.

The Warrior

H e sat meditating in his room, his socks off, his
legs crossed, as sunlight cut diagonally around him. He
lived in an abandoned loft, with old wooden floors, and his
room was almost bare of furniture. Sometimes he meditated
silently and other times in a loud howling voice. He meditated on high alpine flowers, Indian Paintbrush and white
Shasta daises, the peaks of the Colorado Rockies. But in
the end he couldn't sustain such thoughts for long before
coming back to her.

They met downtown at the Haymarket. He went there
because the vegetables in the outdoor stalls were as cheap
as they come, five pounds of tomatoes for a dollar, three
big eggplants for the same. He knew the good salesmen,
the ones who wouldn't give him too much rotten food and

whose scales were not a complete lie, and he liked to talk to them. That day, one of the salesmen was telling him about how he used to have a delivery service before he went broke. He was an old Italian, with gray stubble on his face, missing one eye, and his anxious movements only highlighted her more as she stood next to him, waiting patiently, her hair long and blond, straight and spun like gold. It was cold out, a January Saturday morning. He turned from the Italian to observe her, and for some reason she didn't pretend not to notice him. She raised her smooth chin and stared straight at him. She bought two pounds of string beans before he could get his onions, and said, "I'm not who you think I am."

They went to her apartment and had sex all over, standing up and sitting down, across her futon, against the kitchen wall. She said she liked his thick black hair. He knew sleeping with anyone on the first night was a bad omen. When they were done she pulled out a pack of Marlboros and lit up, and although he didn't smoke regularly, he took a cigarette too. They sat on her futon naked, with their backs against the wall.

She was pretty in the unconventional sense of the word, he decided, meaning that she wore no makeup and that her face was unusual, her skin very pale, her eyes blue, teardrop shaped and a little sad. She seemed to have a face which hid more than it revealed, taut cheeks and an angular jaw with secrets restrained behind it.

She took a few drags on her cigarette, inhaled deeply, and blew the smoke gently outward, holding it in so long not much came out. She didn't look at him, only at the small room filled with books and magazines piled in heaps, and said, "How much do you think a horse weighs?"

"What?"

"I said, how much do you think a horse weighs?"

"I don't know. Why?"

"Because I'm curious."

She seemed nervous.

She stood up and went to the kitchen, the back of her legs covered with goose bumps. Her tiny apartment was barely heated. Her arms were long and narrow, which made the tight roundness of her butt even more noticeable. Tired sunlight of late afternoon winter suffused her room. He stood up, naked and cold.

"So how long have you lived here?" he asked. He didn't know what to say.

She opened an old refrigerator, which crouched in the dark and dirty recesses of her small kitchen, and pulled out a couple of eggs from what seemed to be an ancient carton. They were the last two eggs. The fridge held only a few old carrots and a couple of nearly empty jars of jam.

"You like eggs? It's all I have except the string beans."

"Yeah, sure." He wasn't really that hungry.

She turned the flame up to its highest level and cooked the eggs and put a few plates into her cupboards. The lining inside the shelves must have come from twenty years before. He could see chips which revealed previous coats of paint. The eggs fried in the pan and she cooked them for so long and at such high heat without looking at them or at him, and without seeming to look at anything in particular, that the eggs burned. He cleared his throat when the eggs charred after she did nothing to remove them, and she lifted the pan off the flame.

"I hope you don't mind burnt eggs," she said, but she didn't seem to care.

He went back to her room to pick up his faded jeans and his other clothes and food from the market. "I think I'm going to go now. Thanks." It sounded ridiculous to him to say thanks, but he didn't know what else to say.

She cut the eggs in half with a spatula in one quick harsh movement, and when she looked up from the eggs she had a gaunt, paler look on her face. "Why are you going?"

"It seems pretty clear you don't want me here. We just met in the Haymarket."

"No, stay," she said.

And so he stayed.

Later that evening they went to a small, cheap, underground café. Inside they sold used books. Sometimes they had jazz, she said, but she didn't know any of the groups who played, and although she said she liked the place, you couldn't tell that by looking at her face and she told him it had been a long time since she had gone there, or for that matter anywhere much. They found a table for two in the corner, the cellar was crowded. He thought she looked particularly beautiful with her face lit up from a candle on their table. He ordered a cup of tea; it was cheapest. She ordered the same.

"It's warm in here," he said.

"Yeah, it's nice. It's been almost a year since I've had sex with anyone," she said matter-of-factly, almost dryly. He wondered why she would bring something like that up so suddenly, with such restrained emotion.

He reached towards her, placed his hands around the candle ball and said, "Why's that?"

"I don't want to talk about it." She glanced away from him, toward the distant wall, and then continued, "It had to be someone anonymous."

"Like me?"

"You look like the kind someone can confess to and the secret will be secure."

"Lonely?"

"Not necessarily lonely, but alone."

"I live in a warehouse in Roxbury. The building isn't coded for anyone to live there so the landlord rents it to me illegally. I'm the only tenant except for one other guy on the other side of the building."

"That's what I mean," she said. She picked at some candle wax on the table. The room was full of chatter. For a moment they didn't say anything. "Let's get out of here," she said suddenly.

"Why? We haven't even gotten our tea."

"Let's go," she got up. She rushed out, barely pausing to put on her jacket, forgetting her gloves. He scooped them up for her, and when he gave them to her outside she seemed not to notice them, but she put them on and he was glad, at least, that her hands would stay warm.

*

When they got back to her apartment it was completely dark; there was no moon out. A bulb over the stairway up to her apartment spread harsh light into the cracked plaster corners where a few spider webs swayed in the cold currents of wind which came in from the outside.

She had asked him to come home with her; she had insisted, and he wanted to be sure she got home all right.

Inside her apartment she started to cry. Her tears came down slowly. She stood in the center of her room dressed in an old leather coat, her shoulders drooping, her spine slightly bent, her whole body tired and exhausted like someone who has just walked a hundred miles. He tried to soothe her by rubbing her back, but she flinched and pushed him, saying, "Get away." He stepped back and she said, "I'm going to the bathroom." She walked quickly to the toilet, which was just off her bedroom, with great determination. She almost ran to the bathroom, she strode so powerfully. She locked the door on the inside.

"Whatever it is, it will be all right," he said, standing next to the closed door. He placed his ear against the door and heard water rushing. It sounded, alternately, like she was sobbing and then brushing her teeth. He calmed down when he heard the brushing and walked around the room.

She had all sorts of books with photos of every kind of painting and sculpture: pictures of Korean pottery and modern paintings by Max Beckmann, Chuck Close, and Lucian Freud. Every book was used, the paper covers tattered and worn. On top of one pile he saw a photo of a statue of a strange Chinese horse, all green and white glazed, leaping through the air with an immense warrior riding on top, the warrior's arm pulled back in battle as a spear from another soldier went into the horse's side. How heavy would the horse feel if it fell on top of the warrior?

The sound of great globs of water rushing into a bathtub and into the sink came from behind the bathroom door. What was she doing in there? Maybe he should go and leave her alone. She didn't really know him or want *him*; he could be anyone, anyone at all and to her it would all be the same.

"Are you all right?" he said. He put his ear against the door to the bathroom. It was hard to tell what was going on inside just by the sounds. He heard mainly water falling into a bathtub and a little splashing. "I think I'm going to go now."

"No, stay." The sound of her voice behind all of the water almost surprised him. Her voice was frail.

"Do you need anything?"

"You can come in now," she said faintly.

He tried the door but it was still locked. "I can't."

"I know."

"So how can I come in?"

"You have to come in with just your mind."

He wasn't quite sure what that meant, but he tried to imagine himself coming into the bathroom and seeing her naked in the tub. He would sit on the toilet seat and look at her in the bathtub, all skinny and frail in the green water, and listen to her.

"Are you inside now?" she asked. She turned off the water and he heard her much better. The only sound came from an occasional drip.

"Yes."

"I want to tell you about Michael," she said. "He was my fiancé. We were going to get married a year ago."

"I would never have imagined you to be the marrying type." He tried to sound unconcerned, to speak in a normal conversational style.

"I know. But we were going to get married."

"And what happened?"

"We knew each other from high school. He was completely different from me." Her voice echoed in the tiled walls of her bathroom. She splashed some water violently. "He was a couple of years older, a senior in high school when I was a sophomore. He was always very physical, while I was cerebral. We really didn't have anything in common except he lived on the same block as me and I'd known him since kindergarten. We didn't even start to fool around or to spend much time with each other until late high school. But somehow, the proximity . . . and I guess he had always looked at me. He claims he used to come over to the jungle gym when he was in third grade, and when I was in first, just to watch me hang upside down with my skirt flopping over.

"In any case, we became very serious, and when he graduated from high school he joined the Army. He always had a crew cut and his father had been in the military— although he had left them when he was about twelve. But he'd always idolized his father, and I guess that's why he wanted to go into the Army, although I don't think his father had ever been much of a soldier. He was mainly an alcoholic. Are you following me?"

"Yes."

She spoke in an even voice, nearly a monotone of restrained emotion.

"So when Michael signed up he went off for training, and I was very sad and confused. I wasn't even done with high school yet, and none of my friends could understand what I was doing with a military type, and that made his going all the harder since there was no one to share the loss of him with. He went to Fort Dix, and it turned out he was a crack A-1 shooter, a real Robin Hood or William Tell. They put him in a special sniper unit, and a little after he was done with training they sent him to Saudi Arabia for the invasion of Iraq, and he led the vanguard in."

"You mean he fought in the Gulf?"

He was surprised at where events were taking them, at where the conversation was going. So she hadn't been alone the whole time, she wasn't really like *him*, he thought.

"They sent him in before any of the tank units, before any of the other waves. He was in the first assault, and he was really good at what he did, and his whole unit moved over the dunes, he told me, and they wasted anything they found. They moved like they were on a meat conveyor belt in a processing plant. He would always tell me how he cut one man in two, completely in half, with a high powered machine gun mounted on his jeep. He was the gunner, and they came on a group of Iraqis, and the Air Force was dropping in laser-guided missiles just ahead of them, and he picked out one man who was running towards him— even though he seemed completely unarmed—and he didn't know what took over him, but he just cut that man in two with his machine gun, tat tat tat tat tat, Michael would always say."

"Jesus."

"And when he came home, he didn't want to talk about it much at first, and then all he wanted to do was talk about the burnt bodies and the enemy's melded weapons and the incredible force of our weapons. And he would wake up in the middle of the night, and I would wake up with him and tell him 'It's going to be all right, you'll see.' And I would rub his forehead and get him some orange juice or water. But it was hard, and he didn't want to do anything; he didn't want to report to his National Guard unit—he had switched when he came back—and he didn't even want to sit in the sun when it was a nice sunny day. But finally, I was making some progress in college studying art, and I said, 'Let's get married.' And he said, 'Why, what's the point?' But he agreed at last, and so we made the preparations—"

She stopped. "So we made the preparations. And that's when—" her voice turned higher. "That's when he left the apartment one day, just before our wedding, and he killed himself. He jumped off the Longfellow bridge into the Charles River in the middle of winter."

If he could, he would go to her now and hold her.

He wanted to open the door and let her cry with him just holding her, with her swaying like a baby in his arms, rocking gently until calmness and sleep.

"I'm sorry," she said. "I needed to tell you. I needed to tell someone. I'm all alone now," she said, and she began to sob.

"I'm glad you told me." He felt tears coming to his eyes. "I'm all alone, too," he said, yet so quietly he thought she might not be able to hear him, but he couldn't find the strength to make his voice which was gravelly now with sadness louder. "Can I come in now?"

"Yes," she said. He couldn't wait to hold her tight, to hold her while she cried, her body wet and naked and warm from the water of the bathtub, and weak yet maybe purged and no longer alone. She turned the key, and the bolt sounded heavier than he had anticipated. It was an old lock, heavy and somehow backward looking; it seemed to be a relic from the past stronger than the future. She opened the door a crack, and he came into the white tiled bathroom. She splashed back into the tub as he entered. She looked as pale as the snows of January outside. The water was not, as he had assumed, warm. It was icy blue, and she was white and blue too, the veins of her body streaking up her neck. The bathroom was clammy, the bathtub a frozen lake. "I'm sorry to do this to you," she said, and she crouched in a ball at the back of the tub with her knees drawn in close up to her chest, to her breasts. "I'm really sorry," she said, and then she blew a hole through her head.

*

He sat alone in his room in the dark. What would it mean to not be alone? How would it feel? It had been so long.

Sometimes at night he walked the more or less deserted streets of his neighborhood. The old warehouse that he lived in, a giant brick box, was surrounded by a high chain-link fence with razor wire.

He decided to go for a walk.

It had been two months now since he had met her, and he hadn't even known her then. The area around his warehouse was full of garbage, left over junk from a Chinese food company which sometimes rented the warehouse and which left wooden crates, paper, and tin lying around. He kicked a few pieces of tin and opened the chain-link fence. Down the street there was an old boarded-up liquor store and past that a gas station with rusting pumps. He walked by the gas station and saw the attendant inside his bullet-proof chamber, smoking a cigarette, watching a tiny black and white TV. The mercury lights were so bright his eyes felt uncomfortable, and he moved on into the darker neighborhoods of row houses. The air was musty and cold; it was warm enough to think that spring might come, but that was just Mother Nature fooling him; it was still winter. He walked further down side alleys until he was completely enveloped by solitude and darkness. He stood in the middle of a narrow street filled with old decaying row houses and looked around him. Flashing colors of televisions flickered from many otherwise dark rooms, up and down the block. Each house was a cocoon. It was cold out, but he stood in the center of the street for a long time, until his toes were almost frozen. He looked at each house, wanting to know who lived inside, wanting to know who was behind each door, who owned each dog that sometimes barked in the dog houses behind the wooden picket and chain-linked front fences. I will stay here until I run into someone, he thought. But no one came. So he walked back to the gas station to speak to the attendant, and he bought a pack of Marlboros.

About the author

Joshua Barkan

Joshua Barkan was born in California in 1969. He spent much of his childhood abroad, living in Kenya, Tanzania, France and India. After attending Yale University, where he was awarded writing fellowships, he spent a year teaching in Japan. He is a graduate of the Iowa Writers Workshop and now lives with his wife in Boston. *Before Hiroshima* is his first published collection of stories.

The fonts used in this book are from the Garamond, Lydian and Gill families.